Beautiful Liars

AUG

Books by Kylie Adams

FLY ME TO THE MOON

BABY, BABY

EX-GIRLFRIENDS

BEAUTIFUL LIARS

THE ONLY THING BETTER THAN CHOCOLATE
(with Janet Dailey and Sandra Steffen)

SANTA BABY
(with Lisa Jackson, Elaine Coffman and Lisa Plumley)

Published by Kensington Publishing Corporation

Beautiful Liars

Kylie Adams

K

KENSINGTON BOOKS
http://www.kensingtonbooks.com

ISBN-13: 978-0-7582-0500-1
ISBN-10: 0-7582-0500-7

First Printing: October 2008
10 9 8 7 6 5 4 3 2 1

Printed in the United States of America

ACKNOWLEDGMENTS

For my brothers . . .

Tim Salem—He's one by blood. What would I do without the guy who calls just to remind me that Maureen McGovern hasn't had a hit since "The Morning After" (love theme from *The Poseidon Adventure*)? The best New Year's Eve ever: ditching a party and staying home with Tim to watch *New Year's Rockin' Eve* with Dick Clark. We ended up changing the channel to witness a Louise Mandrell concert on another network, then spent the rest of the night mocking her mangled version of "Auld Lang Syne."

Ricky Santoyo—He's one by marriage. This guy was poor as dirt and drove my sister off to Texas in a raggedy pickup truck five minutes after she graduated college. Now he's got his own commercial signage empire and zips around in a Porsche. Call him Cinderfella.

Kenny Nolan—He's one by marriage, too. I was sold when I saw the official engagement photo—sister was impossibly gorgeous, diamonds gleaming, future brother-in-law naturally tan and movie star handsome. Then I discover he's a real-life MacGyver. Once he got me back on the road when my clunky old Mercedes (I've since upgraded) broke down. And Ken fixed it with just a pen and the string from a Neiman Marcus shopping bag!

Men are such a combination of good and evil.
                                                    —Jackie Kennedy

THE IT PARADE
BY JINX WIATT

Fill in the Blanks

All the spa pampering in the world couldn't console that aging TV news diva. Her creep of a boyfriend broke up with her via FedEx letter—delivered while she was recovering from plastic surgery. Paging bastard of the century! Think it can't get any worse? Read on, darlings. Apparently, it was *her* hormone specialist who got his sexual equipment back in working order. Just so he could use it on a much younger woman. Oh, and by the way, his current flame and his most recent ex will be co-hosting a new talk show this fall. I'd give up my first born to be a fake eyelash in that makeup room.

1
Sutton

"It's *my* party, and I'll bitch if I want to," Sutton Lancaster snapped.

She was fifty. She was furious. And she was so fucking hot. Burning up, in fact. Actual sweat trickled between her breasts, as if a water faucet had been attached there. Goddamn hot flashes.

A nervous-looking Jay Lufkin stared back at her. "Hey, it's your night."

"Is that so?" Sutton challenged him.

"You're the birthday girl. You're the star. Bitch away. Who's going to stop you?" Jay downed the last of his Pom-Pom, glancing around for a waiter to take his empty glass.

Sutton glowered. The mere sight of this smooth-faced overachiever—smug, ageless, and all-knowing in that Tucker Carlson sort of way—only exasperated her irritation. Here she stood, a news *star* with no real power, dateless at a party celebrating her half-century mark, and sick from an hors d'oeuvre binge twenty minutes ago. Of this much she was certain: Oprah had done fifty with considerably more panache.

She surveyed the Roof scene at Soho House New York, a private members club and hotel in Manhattan's Meatpacking

District. Labor Day had come and gone. Everybody was back from the Hamptons. But the poolside theme still had the assorted revelers behaving like summer might never end.

Sutton silently noted that nobody from Fox News had bothered to show up. How gracious. She expected as much from the network prima donnas. But what about all those little right-wing bitches and bastards that had glommed onto her for mentoring? Where were they? She tried to push the snub out of her mind. Who needed the assholes?

Every staffer at America's number one cable news network was probably putting money on how long it would take Sutton Lancaster to join the scrap heap of forgotten talking heads who left a good thing in search of more screen time and a higher profile.

Sutton took in the fantastic views of the West Village and the Hudson River, zoning out the cacophonous party chatter and the unimpressive turntable skills of computer-heiress-turned-DJ Panda Dell. Wow. The girl could put the needle on a Nelly Furtado record. Big fucking deal.

Her thoughts zeroed in on the bigger deal at the moment—her own career. There were times (like right now) when she stopped to ask herself, *Why are you doing a high wire act at the age of fifty?*

The answer was simple. A woman could either take the leap or wait for the ax. Because the latter was inevitable. No matter how many times they told her otherwise, Sutton knew the truth. Internal support for her had eroded long ago. Now it was mere ambivalence. And there were whispers of concern . . . *about her age.* Rumors were rampant regarding a secret memo being shared among executives that ranked the "fuckability factor" of all on-air female talent.

We Report. You Decide. Viewers actually believed that pickup line. Several years ago Sutton had fallen for a come-on far worse: *We're going to make you a star.*

The Fox suits sure knew how to court a girl. But back then, Sutton would have been an easy mark for career attention of any kind. Hell, she might have been tempted to jump into bed with the public access channel.

Oh, God, it was a bitter pill to swallow—the realization that she had lived out an entire career standing on the precipice of something bigger and better that never came. Anyone who said that it just took talent, drive, and tenacity to make your dreams come true was a liar. Or an idiot. Because the two secret ingredients for real success were luck and timing.

To the untrained eye, Sutton had *made it*, leapfrogging from large market affiliate to larger market affiliate on her way to grab the brass ring of every broadcast news anchor: a place on one of the big networks.

Ultimately, she darkened the doorways of every one, doing the substitute rounds on weekend newscasts, pulling correspondent duties on news magazine shows, listening patiently as executive after executive fed her cast-off lines like, "Hang in there. We're grooming you for a major slot. But you have to pay your dues."

Then Fox News had come to the door with flowers, saying all the right things. *We need a trusted, recognizable female anchor. You deserve to be a household name.*

So she jumped ship. *Again.* And nothing happened. *Again.* Once more, Sutton Lancaster got lost in the shuffle. Bill O'Reilly was Fox's Superman. Sean Hannity was taking off, too. Then the network poached Greta Van Susteren from CNN and gave her massive promotion with a cushy prime-time slot, relegating Sutton to more fill-in duties and the standard-issue ego stroke—her own Sunday afternoon week-in-review show.

And then, after years of low profile misery, she met Jay Lufkin, a producer with White Glove Entertainment. His call came like most life-altering calls do—from out of the blue. They met for lunch at Nooch, a Japanese-Thai noodle bar, and he told her about *The Beehive*, a new television project in development with her in mind as top-billed host.

"It's a multicultural version of *The View*," Jay had pitched.

And at that moment, Sutton had wanted to get up and leave. But the ramen bowl was too tasty, and she was just starting to feel the tom yumtini cocktail. So she resisted the urge to bolt.

She thought about this producer's copycat pipe dream to muscle in on the vehicle that had turned Star Jones into a media monster and then publicly killed the beast to make room for Rosie, and after that headline-hogging train wreck, Whoopi Goldberg and Sherri Shepherd.

The View made it look easy. Put some women around a table. Watch them yack it up. But it was anything but easy. That's why almost every imitator had crashed and burned. *Painfully*. What separated Jay's idea from those debacles?

"Our show is called *The Beehive*," Jay had told her. "And you would be the Queen Bee."

Right away, she wanted to hear more. "Go on."

"Imagine yourself flanked by a Black American Princess and a gay man that every woman watching will wish was her best friend." He paused a beat, smiling. "How's that for diversity?"

Sutton had experienced an electric tingle. This had real potential. A gut thing told her so.

"We've compiled a short list," Jay continued. "Simone Williams and Finn Robards are the front-runners."

Sutton's brain computer went to work. Both names rang a bell. Simone was an ex-model and bit player actress, though more famous lately for dumping New York Yankee Tommy

Robb before the ball dropped last New Year's Eve. Nine months later and the gossip columns were still sorting out the messy details.

As for Finn Robards, he was a trust fund baby and society It Boy, always turning up in Page Six, *W*, *Gotham*, and *Hamptons* at some glamorous event.

Jay seemed to pick up on her interest, because he moved in for the kill by launching into his own *A&E Biography*. Loved talk shows as a kid. Lived for *The Merv Griffin Show*. Produced his own version in the backyard using neighbors as guests. Interned with Regis Philbin. Worked in various capacities with Joan Rivers, Ricki Lake, Queen Latifah, and Maury Povich before joining White Glove Entertainment.

Instinctively, Sutton knew that Jay Lufkin had talent. He might be pushing forty, but deep down, he was still that dorky kid pretending to be Merv Griffin. She could see the passion in his eyes. This guy was so desperate to step out of the shadows and run his own show that he would do whatever necessary to make it successful—or die trying.

But Sutton had the most to lose here. She was hard news. This was entertainment fluff. And to say rolling the dice with daytime syndication could be a precarious career move was the understatement of the century. If it tanked, what then? Once she stepped into the alternate universe of talking about holiday fashions for Paris Hilton's exotic pet of the moment, she could hardly go back to lobbing serious questions about homeland security.

To a degree, what Sutton knew about White Glove tempered her anxiety. The young company had managed three successful launches in the past year—a female-targeted celebrity game show called *Bunko Night*, a reality series about young nurses, and *Sexually Aware*, a provocative hour hosted by former-porn-star-turned-sex-therapist Ashlyn Saint. All were reaching at least ninety percent of American households and posting record ratings in key demographics.

"White Glove is very selective about the properties it chooses to develop," Jay had told her. "They have sophisticated methods of researching and testing concepts. Feedback on *The Beehive* is already incredible. And it's still in the early stages of development."

Sutton had just stared at Jay, recalling the *Media Week* profile on Ashlyn Saint that detailed her shrewd profit participation deal. That whore would end up making millions. "I'll want an executive producer credit and an ownership stake in the show," she said.

That had been months ago. And now, on the eve of the program's launch, with stations and time slots secured, the publicity juggernaut under way, the staff assembled, the major guests booked, and the creative vision determined, word came down from top executives at White Glove that Sutton, Simone, and Finn were not quite enough.

Some last minute testing revealed that *The Beehive* needed a fourth host buzzing about. A relatable personality for the coveted young female viewers. Christ. At the end of the day, it always came down to age. Working in television *never* let you forget how old you were.

"Happy birthday!" Simone cooed, leaning in to offer air kisses on each cheek.

The intrusion sent Sutton crashing back to her own party. It was, after all, her fucking birthday. "Don't remind me."

"Why?" Simone cried, glancing around appreciatively. "This night is fantastic. And everybody knows that fifty is the new forty."

Sutton stopped to wonder. What would be fair punishment for girls under thirty who made such pronouncements?

Immediate death came to mind. And if that seemed too harsh, at least facial disfigurement.

"You look amazing," Simone went on. "I *love* the dress. It's Marc Jacobs, right?"

Sutton nodded, self-consciously fingering the oversized ruffles cascading down the left side of the slim silhouette. Was it too much? Did she look ridiculous? Could she still pull off sleeveless? Yes, she worked out like a demon, but no matter how hard she tried, there was still that slight jiggle of under-arm flesh.

And here stood Simone Williams, impossibly beautiful, young, and thin, a vision of caramel loveliness, so unfussy in her black, one-shouldered evening dress by Prada, accessorized by a sturdy leather belt and a flirty Louis Vuitton Damier Sauvage bag. She didn't wear the look. She carried it. Everything about her—the hair, the clothes, the makeup—was a beacon of effort-less perfection. So naturally, Sutton wanted to kill the bitch.

Simone swayed to the beat of Michael Bublé's "Save the Last Dance for Me," popping a slender hip toward Jay. "You look like you're feeling no pain. How many have you had?"

Jay grinned blankly, bleary-eyed, close to being all the way gone.

"Enough to wake up in anyone's bed but his own," Finn remarked, swooping in to kiss Sutton on the cheek. "Happy birthday, diva. How old are you? Twenty-nine again?"

She embraced him warmly, whispering "Fuck you," into his diamond-studded ear. Something told her that Finn Robards might be *The Beehive*'s secret weapon. He had a rare quality that rendered him infinitely appealing, a special brand of in-souciance.

Sutton had never known a man who smelled better. Morning, noon, or night, his intoxicating scent never faltered. And he was sexy as hell, the exact sort of charismatic gay man who could infiltrate a straight couple's life, captivating the girl and titillating the guy.

As Sutton stood there with Simone and Finn, the reality did not escape her. Where only days ago they had been a signed and sealed triumvirate, they were now an incomplete quartet. The announcement to add another host had done a number on all of them. Nothing like a clarion call from the top to say, "This isn't working."

Finn cleared his throat. "Well, ladies, I know who the fourth Supreme is."

Sutton fumed silently. If Finn knew this information, then Jay knew it, too. Son of a bitch. She glared at him. "Why are you holding out on me?"

Jay held up his Pom-Pom. "I had every intention of telling you tonight. I just wanted to have enough to drink first."

"It's that bad?" Simone asked. "Oh, my God. Is it a fat person?"

Finn fixed a stare on Sutton. There was an apology in his eyes. "You may as well hear this now. It leads Jinx Wiatt's column tomorrow."

"Who is it?" Sutton demanded, bracing herself for the impact.

Finn looked at Jay, then back to Sutton. "Emma Ronson."

The announcement knocked the breath from Sutton's body. Jay shut his eyes and liquored up even more.

"Isn't that the girl from *Today in New York*?" Simone asked. Finn nodded.

"Wait a minute," Simone continued, glancing from Finn to Sutton and back again as she put it all together. Suddenly, her gorgeous hazel eyes went wide. "Isn't she dating . . ."

"I need a break from this heat," Sutton murmured, darting away before Simone could finish. She slipped down to the fourth floor White Room, grateful for the air-conditioning. Was it really so hot outside? Or was it her hormones again? Her therapy needed an adjustment. First order of business to-morrow—call Dr. Barak.

Thank God for the Israeli gynecologist, a founding member of the controversial American Academy of Anti-Aging Medicine. For long, frustrating years Sutton had suffered intermittent fatigue, depression, itching, vaginal dryness, and a diminished sex drive. She blamed her miseries on everything—work stress, lack of sleep, emotional upturns from one lousy relationship after another. But then a colleague at Fox had told her about Dr. Barak.

He diagnosed her immediately as being in hormonal chaos and calibrated a bio-identical cocktail to her individual chemical needs. In the beginning, it was tough. Sore breasts from too much estrogen, fogginess from too much progesterone, and a nasty round of acne from too much testosterone. But Dr. Barak dialed down the dosages, found her optimal levels, and the results were suddenly amazing.

Sutton could finally sleep through the night. She had more confidence. She could concentrate, actually sit down and read a book chapter by chapter without veering off into a private Mars.

Her sex drive returned with a vengeance, too, and with her thicker hair, perkier breasts, and harder nails, she finally lived out the secret fantasy of fucking the hot UPS driver who had been delivering packages to her co-op for the last three years.

Of course, this kind of therapy was costing her a small fortune—easily a thousand dollars per month. But Sutton would pay twice that amount or even more for such blissful relief.

She adored Dr. Barak. His voice was soothing, his demeanor patient and sympathetic. He listened to her problems and symptoms, instead of just shoving a prescription for antidepressants into her hand and moving on to the next patient. That was the course of treatment for so many of those white-coat bastards.

With no screening scheduled in the Cinema, the White Room was deserted. Sutton dimmed the lights and sought sanctuary on one of the sofas, stretching out, relishing the peace and quiet, thankful to be off her feet.

The tranquil moment lasted no more than a nanosecond. That bitch's name was smoking inside her brain. *Emma Ronson*.

Sutton closed her eyes, attempting to breathe, trying to relax. Oh, God, how she needed a dab of progesterone right now. Just one drop under her tongue. Enough to equalize her stress level.

A girlish giggle invaded the silence.

"Come on, nobody's in here," a male voice whispered thickly.

"No, let's go back to the party."

"In a minute. I want to show you something first."

"What?"

"This."

There was a muffled giggle. And then the unmistakable sound of lips and tongues in full erotic battle.

Sutton rose slightly to see the young couple braced against the mirrored bar. She started to leave.

"Whose party is this anyway?" the girl asked.

"I don't know. Some old news chick. The event planner called my publicist and said she needed bodies at this thing. Nobody wanted to come. I figure the drinks are free, and I might get laid. Why not?"

Sutton sank back down and just lay there, frozen. She had stopped breathing after hearing *old news chick*.

"Oh, I know her!" the girl exclaimed. "She's the woman wearing that stupid white dress."

The guy chuckled. "The fossilized bitch with all the ruf-fles?"

"Yeah. That's Sutton Lancaster."

"Really? Wouldn't know. I get my news off the Net."

"I feel sorry for her."

"Feel sorry for this."

A moan. More kissing.

"I'm serious. Didn't you hear? She was dating this guy. He broke up with her by FedEx and hooked up with Emma Ronson."

"The *Today in New York* hottie? Now I *know* who she is."

"What's that guy's name? My friend Nicole used to date him . . . Garrison Friedberg. That's it." She giggled again. "Have you heard of him? He's this old rich Jew. Nicole says he's got a huge cock, but it only gets semi-hard."

"Unlike mine. Which right now is all the way hard."

"Shut up. All you think about is sex."

"So? I'll think about other stuff when I can only get *semi-hard.*"

"That's wrong, don't you think? Breaking up with some-one by FedEx. Would you ever do that to a girl?"

"Fuck no. FedEx is expensive. I'd just send her an e-mail." He laughed at his own joke.

The girl was laughing, too. "You're such a dick."

"Speaking of dicks . . ."

"I still can't believe that *Emma Ronson* is with that guy. I mean, her last boyfriend was Dean Paul Lockhart. How do you go from him . . . to *that*?"

"Baby, you're killing me here. Please do something else with your mouth."

"Seriously. Dean Paul is, like, gorgeous. And Garrison is . . . well, he's just gross."

"Women are different," the guy reasoned. "They can get

into big, sweaty lugs with no problem. As long as they're rich. I guess girls figure, 'Okay, he doesn't look so great, he's not so sexy, but at least he's got a yacht!'"

"Did you notice her face?" the girl asked.

"Whose face?"

"Sutton Lancaster!"

"Not really. I couldn't make it out for all the fucking ruffles."

The girl giggled. "You can tell she's had work done. Her brows are arched, and her eyes are upturned like a cat's. Isn't that sad? To be competing with a girl almost half your age for some sweaty old man? I'd rather just die already."

"I'm about to."

"About to what?"

"Die if you don't blow me in the next thirty seconds!"

"Okay, okay. God, you're such a pig."

And then came the rustle of a zipper, the guy's moaning and rapid breathing, the girl's slurping ministrations . . .

Sutton Lancaster just lay there, immobile in the dark, feeling the heat of humiliation. It was burning her cheeks. It was making her eyes glitter with tears.

Goddamn turning fifty! Goddamn this Marc Jacobs dress! Goddamn Garrison Friedberg! Sutton knew about his semi-hard cock firsthand. Every erectile dysfunction pill on the market made him sick, so she had sent him to Dr. Barak, who put him on a therapy that made him as rigid and horny as a rock star after a sold-out concert. And then he used it on the first younger woman he could find.

Emma Ronson.

The bitch had taken her boyfriend. And now the bitch was moving in on her show. Situations like this could best be described in one little word.

War.

And as far as Sutton Lancaster was concerned, it was on.

THE IT PARADE
BY JINX WIATT

Fill in the Blanks

How do you mend a broken heart? For a certain young morning news starlet, recovery is an extreme life makeover. First she traded a young, hard-bodied heir for an old, soft-bodied self-made mogul. Now she's saying good-bye to a serious news career for a silly daytime gabfest. But a close source dishes that all the changes have done little to boost her spirits. The womanizing prince cut her loose because of her position on children (she wanted them; he preferred to wait). But then he got married, and his *fruit*-tastic new baby has become a Manhattan mascot. Now comes word that her new geriatric bed-warmer wants nothing to do with little things that go wah-wah in the night, so much so that he had a vasectomy years ago and has failed to fess up to the fact. This beauty just can't win.

2

Emma

Is it cheating to think about your ex-boyfriend's cock while your current boyfriend is inside you?

Emma Ronson wondered this as Garrison Friedberg pumped away on top of her, thrusting off-rhythm and breathing like an out-of-shape jogger in one-hundred-degree heat.

Dean Paul Lockhart possessed a smaller dick but far more finesse. She missed his amazing corkscrew motion that had never failed to send her to the moon and back.

Garrison was swinging the kind of equipment that male porn stars might envy, but the sexual talent ended there. He just shoved it in, and a few minutes later rolled off her body and over to his side of the bed, completely spent and damp with sweat.

Emma sighed with relief disguised as satisfaction. Making love to Garrison did not exactly hurt, but the thickness and length of him caused intermittent discomfort.

"You've never had a cock as big as mine, have you?"

"No," Emma murmured, her mind drifting as she answered the same question that he asked each and every time.

The gnawing sense of dread was still attacking her insides. Had she made the right move in leaving *Today in New York*?

Emma was weekday coanchor on a proven, top-rated program for the NBC-owned News Channel Four. And she was ditching that for an unproven syndicated daytime venture that could be branded a failure after its debut airing. High stakes career gambling to be sure.

Garrison reached out to stroke her inner thigh.

Emma glanced down and noticed that his nails needed clipping. She pushed the thought away. Somehow he made up for all of his failings with a certain blustery charm.

The telephone jangled.

Emma glanced over to see that it was Delilah Krause calling. She picked up the cordless and slipped out of bed, making a beeline for the bathroom to retrieve a robe. "Hi," she whispered.

"I *hate* Ivy League boys," Delilah announced without preamble. "Have I mentioned that?"

"Only every day," Emma murmured.

Delilah was a featured player and writer on the Comedy Central sketch series, *Laugh Track*. She had recently been hailed in the pages of *Entertainment Weekly* as the next Tina Fey. No matter, the show's boys club mentality behind the scenes was still slow to catch up.

"You sound sleepy," Delilah said. "Did I wake you?"

"No, no, of course not," Emma insisted in a hushed tone.

"Why are you whispering?"

"I'm not . . . Garrison's here."

"You just had sex!" Delilah accused.

Emma sighed.

Delilah laughed. "Be careful. Men his age are supposed to nap in the middle of the day. You could kill him."

"Oh, I think he'll kill me first."

"Have you picked up the *Post* today?"

"That sounds like a warning not to."

"Trust me. It is."

"Okay, I'll steer clear."

"Good girl."

"I don't even care what's in there. I believe you when you say it's something I don't want to see." Emma paused a beat. "Okay, what is it?"

Delilah groaned. "More of the same. Those two gorgeous twits and their idiot child."

Emma bit down on her lower lip. As much as she might loathe herself for it later, today's edition of the *New York Post* would be in her hands within a matter of minutes.

Having a famous boyfriend sucked something fierce. Because once he becomes an *ex-boyfriend* (as most boyfriends do) there is still no escaping him. And Emma had a personal case study in this observation . . . *Dean Paul Lockhart.*

He was the closest thing to a prince that America had to offer, the son of a celebrated New York senator and a retired big screen actress who walked away from Hollywood while still at the top of the A-list. As their only child, he became a household name at birth, a celebrated baby and toddler, an adored boy, a scrutinized teenager, and an obsessively chronicled young man.

Like every other straight single woman in Manhattan, Emma had followed Dean Paul Lockhart's romantic entanglements in the columns with hopeful interest. Even so, his quickie marriage to Aspen Bauer, a former cast member of MTV's *The Real World*, should have been ample warning.

But Emma had succumbed to Dean Paul's devastating good looks and laconic charms at a cocktail party for a new perfume launch. Talking turned to making out. A one night fling upgraded to a long weekend. Suddenly, they were living together and making vague plans for the future.

Until the subject of children floated up to the surface.

Emma had been approaching thirty, and seeing so many women just beyond that age struggling with infertility, she wanted to start a family sooner rather than later. But Dean Paul preferred to wait . . . *indefinitely*.

The conflict sealed the fate of the relationship. And as if to accelerate its demise, Dean Paul morphed into a complete asshole during the final months, making it easier for Emma to leave him.

Of course, the real heartbreak hit a short time later. The man who could not commit was suddenly ready for marriage again. His engagement to Tilly Winston, the ubiquitous heiress, cosmetics model, and junior social fixture, generated exhaustive attention. This continued all the way up to the wedding.

And then, just months into the marriage, the man who wanted to wait to have children, announced that he and his wife were expecting their first baby, a girl. The news sent Emma into a deep depression, a condition that left her vulnerable to the head-scratching appeal of Garrison Friedberg.

He was the self-proclaimed magalog king of Manhattan, a man on the cutting edge of hybrid publications that combined elements of a magazine and a catalogue. Garrison knew how to finely doctor the editorial mix to control the message and create a brand world. His clients included top retailers and designers like Bergdorf Goodman, Neiman Marcus, Tory Burch, Kate Spade, and Donatella Versace.

Garrison was not quite handsome, not quite in shape, but quite old enough to be Emma's father. Still, there was a sexiness about him, a worldly, baby-I've-lived-a-full-life attitude that captivated her. He had approached her on the street with a simple, "You're beautiful. Have dinner with me tonight."

It became a distraction that saved her from the daily despair of reading about Dean Paul and Tilly's newborn child, whom they had christened Cantaloupe. Apparently, they suffered from the Chronic Stupid Name Syndrome that afflicted so many other celebrities. There was Gwyneth Paltrow's Apple, Claudia Schiffer's Casper, Toni Braxton's Denim, John Mellencamp's Speck Wildhorse, Nicolas Cage's Kal-el, and former Spice Girl Geri Halliwell's Bluebell Madonna to name only a few. And now there was Cantaloupe Lockhart.

Just having Garrison around to occasionally fawn over her provided enough emotional succor to persevere through the baby crisis. Suddenly, before Emma even fully realized it, she found herself involved in another relationship. Dean Paul's heat had been replaced by Garrison's comfort. It was hardly perfect. But it was not the worst thing in the world, either.

Emma thought this as she closed the door to the bathroom and turned on the faucet at the sink to drown out the sound of her voice. "Delilah, what the fuck am I doing?"

"I assume you're referring to your life in general," Delilah answered glibly. "This is why I don't recommend sex with old men. It makes a girl too existential."

Emma slumped down onto the edge of the bathtub. "I can predict the rest of my day. As soon as I hang up with you, I'm going to rush out and buy the *Post*. Then I'm going to stare at Dean Paul and that bitch and that perfect baby and be twisted up in knots for the rest of the day."

"So do something different," Delilah reasoned.

"I'm not sure that I want to," Emma said quietly, reflecting on how much power Dean Paul still seemed to have over her life. Once upon a time, she had been an unstoppable force—a high school overachiever, a double degree earner at the University of Miami, a fast riser in the broadcast journalism ranks. And now she had become this simpering girl who could not move past a busted love affair.

The breakup predicated almost everything that she did. Her decision to go into therapy, her reliance on antidepressants, her zombielike openness to an affair with Garrison, even her career shift from a serious journalist on *Today in New York* to a lightweight chatterbox on *The Beehive*. In some way, all of it stemmed from Dean Paul.

"Emma, you have to snap out of this," Delilah said, her voice teeming with equal parts shoulder to cry on and tough love advocacy. "He's not worth it."

"I know," Emma moaned, frustrated by her unwillingness to move forward. God, she was getting on her *own* nerves.

"You need a hot guy to give you a little amnesia. Someone sexier and more famous than Dean Paul. What about Matthew McConaughey?"

Emma cracked a smile. "Do you have his number?"

Delilah sighed. "No, but even if I did, I wouldn't give it to you. He's *my* fantasy."

"Fine," Emma sniffed. "Just don't expect me to share Patrick Dempsey."

"Oh, you bitch. I forgot about him. Let's trade."

"Never," Emma teased.

"So have you checked on Garrison since you bumped uglies?" Delilah asked. "Is he still breathing?"

"You make him sound ancient," Emma protested with good humor. "I'm not exactly Anna Nicole."

"But he *has* voted for over ten presidents."

In her own personal record, Emma could count only three elections. Disturbed by the thought, she shook it away. "I should go. I don't hear Garrison snoring."

"Maybe he's dead," Delilah cracked.

"Oh, that's nice," Emma said, laughing in spite of herself as she hung up and ventured back into the bedroom, where Garrison was alive and well and reading *The Financial Times*.

His gaze zeroed in on the cordless telephone. "Secret boyfriend?"

"Delilah," Emma confirmed.

Garrison grunted disagreeably and returned to his newspaper. There had been one get-acquainted-with-my-friend-Delilah dinner at Mr. Chow. It had not gone well. In fact, he had referred to her as a "foul-mouthed cunt" in the cab on the way home.

Emma began to dress quickly in a Juicy Couture suit that was hanging carelessly across her vanity chair.

"Are we finished?" Garrison asked. Engrossed in an article, he barely looked up. "I could go at it again."

"I have to run down to the newsstand. Can I bring you back anything?"

He shook his head. "Fix me a bourbon before you go."

The request irritated her. It sounded like a line from an old Harold Robbins novel. The rich bastard had just screwed the young girl, and now he expected her to serve him like a geisha. She took in the sight of his bald head and protruding stomach, experiencing a moment's pure disgust.

All of a sudden, it was astonishing that Garrison Friedberg had landed someone like her. Even Sutton Lancaster, a woman closer to his own age, should have been out of his league, not to mention the scores of beautiful girls who had come before both of them.

Men who played the asshole card usually enjoyed consistent success with uneducated women. So why was Emma pouring the Masterpiece bourbon into a highballer instead of splashing it in this guy's face?

The fact that she had no answer simply underscored how far off course she was. Dutifully, Emma delivered the drink.

Garrison accepted it without a word, clicking on the small flat screen television to CNBC's *Street Signs*.

Emma grabbed her BlackBerry and dashed downstairs to the newsstand on the corner. The teaser headline ONE SWEET

LITTLE MELON made her stomach do a revolution as she pushed a dollar into the attendant's hand and walked away, lost in the business of tearing through the smelly newsprint for the actual story.

And there it was. Dean Paul on a stretch of beach in the Hamptons, his body impossibly toned and cut as he cradled Cantaloupe in both arms while a bikini-clad Tilly looked on adoringly.

The impact of the image hit her like a shot to the solar plexus. It was as if someone had stolen the life she always dreamed about, then staged a photograph just to torturously twist the knife.

Her BlackBerry vibrated, followed by the chime of an incoming e-mail. She glanced down to see a message from her agent, Adam Moss. Finally, *The Beehive* deal was negotiated. Contracts were being drawn up. A show prep package would be sent by messenger tonight. She was due on the set tomorrow morning.

A terribly nervous feeling swamped over Emma as she meandered back to her Upper East Side apartment by muscle memory alone. It was the weirdest sensation. She felt estranged from her own life, detached from almost everything.

When she got back, Garrison was in the same position—marooned on her Ralph Lauren mahogany sleigh bed like a beached whale.

"It's official," Emma said quietly. "I'll be cohosting *The Beehive.*"

Garrison glanced up at her curiously. "You sound surprised."

"It's strange," Emma murmured. "Part of me was hoping the negotiations would fall apart. If this doesn't work, I'll be lucky to end up on *Dancing with the Stars.*"

"The show's going to be a hit," Garrison assured her before turning his attention back to the Wall Street talk on CNBC.

She gave him a probing look.

"What?"

"I'm concerned about Sutton."

"We've been over this," Garrison said impatiently. "The tabloids are bullshit. I didn't break up with her by FedEx letter. We ended things on good terms."

His assurance mollified her to a degree.

"But she's difficult as hell on her best day," Garrison went on. "And she might decide to act like a cunt just because you're with me now."

Emma admonished him with narrowed eyes. "I don't like that word."

"Cunt? It's a great word."

"It's offensive."

"Depends on the context," Garrison argued. "If I was fucking you and told you how much I loved your cunt, I bet you'd love the sound of the word."

Emma shook her head. "You're disgusting."

Garrison reached out for her arm and pulled her toward him. "Am I? Fix me another bourbon and come back to bed. I'll show you how disgusting I can be."

Emma went through the motions. She played barmaid. She submitted to his lusty kisses and passionate embraces. But her heart was simply not into it. She wondered if it ever would be again . . . with him . . . or with anyone else.

THE IT PARADE
BY *JINX WIATT*

Fill in the Blanks

Everybody's heard of the poor little rich girl. Well, what about the poor little rich boy? A certain trust fund baby has been put on notice by his fed-up parents that the open credit line days are over. What's an accomplished society boy and aspiring screenwriter to do? Go to work! But at the end of the day, his family might have been better off just extending his allowance. Why? They prefer a low profile for their "confirmed bachelor" son. But he's scored an attention-getting job that insiders are saying will make him a star. That, coupled with his unlikely new BFF, should make poor little rich boy the talk of the town.

3

Finn

"Her poopie doesn't smell bad at all. Isn't that amazing? I mean, have you ever heard of a baby whose poopie didn't stink?" As she waited for an answer, Tilly Lockhart transferred Cantaloupe to the waiting arms of her Russian-born nanny, Veronika.

Finn Robards just stood there, appreciative of the child's uncanny beauty but not convinced that Jo Malone would someday consider concocting a new fragrance based on the baby's shit.

"Well?" Tilly demanded. "Have you ever heard of that?"

"Oh, I thought you were speaking rhetorically," Finn said. "Am I really supposed to answer?"

Tilly rolled her eyes skyward and focused on the nanny. "Veronika, I think Cantaloupe should spend six minutes in her bouncy seat and then take a nice nap." Suddenly, she halted, her violet eyes blazing with anger as she leaned in to sniff the immigrant caregiver. "You're still smoking!"

Veronika's face turned pink with embarrassment. "Mrs. Lockhart . . . I . . . no smoke near—"

Tilly made quite a show out of removing Cantaloupe from

the woman's arms. "I told you to quit! I was very clear about that!"

Veronika turned desperately toward Finn, who had no choice but to look away. After all, what say did he have in the matter?

Tilly cradled Cantaloupe close to her chest and instantly recoiled. "Ugh! Now she needs a bath and another outfit! I can smell your icky smoke on her!"

Veronika started to cry.

"Why are *you* crying, Veronika? Cantaloupe smells like an ashtray, and now I have to reschedule my workout with Paul, which he'll still charge me for, by the way. So expect that to be deducted from your salary this week, assuming you last until the end of it."

"Please, Mrs. Lockart . . . no fire me . . ."

"I'll have to discuss that with Mr. Lockhart," Tilly said primly. "But he's going to be very upset about this. Now please go shower in the guest bathroom. I'll find you something else to wear, so you don't reek of lung cancer. But it'll have to be from Mr. Lockhart's closet, because you're much too large to fit into any of *my* clothes. Honestly, Veronika, this is despicable. I can't have a drug addict caring for my little angel."

Bowing her head in shame, Veronika disappeared from the room.

"Can you believe that?" Tilly hissed. "I think Dean Paul will insist that we fire her."

Finn fought back a laugh. As long as Veronika had not put out a cigarette in Cantaloupe's eye, then her job was safe where Dean Paul was concerned.

"We probably *should* let her go," Tilly went on. "Her sister was tricked into becoming a sex slave in Germany, and

Veronika spends half her days on the Internet searching for her. Have you ever heard anything so ridiculous?" She transferred Cantaloupe over to Finn. "Go to your Uncle Finn, darling, so Mommy can text Mr. Paul."

Finn accepted the precious cargo with great ease, his heart big to bursting as Cantaloupe smiled and giggled at him. Kissing the top of her head and cuddling the bundle close, he could smell nothing but the fresh scent of Bulgari baby wash. The little tot carried not so much as a hint of smoke odor.

Tilly's nimble fingers worked over the BlackBerry keypad. "How will I ever get back to my pre-baby weight with these kind of interruptions?"

In response, Finn simply cast a wayward glance. Standing here just six months after Cantaloupe's birth, Tilly was once again a size zero. But she preferred a state of being slightly less than that. To have a size zero garment taken in a bit by a seamstress gave her an incredible sense of pride.

Tilly completed her text and looked up, smiling at the way Cantaloupe was playing with Finn's nose. "She's such a flirt." One beat. "So did you just stop by to see the most amazing child in the world?"

"That's a bonus. Actually, Dean Paul and I are going to the gym."

Tilly shook her head. "He's on his way to L.A."

"They cancelled the story."

Tilly rolled her eyes. "The wife *is* always the last to know."

"They're slashing the *Hollywood Live* budget left and right. He really sounds worried about his future there."

Tilly nodded vaguely. "What am I going to do about Veronika?"

Finn scolded himself for raising any subject that did not directly orbit around the life and primary concerns of Tilly

Lockhart. "I hear everyone talking about that doctor in Mount Vernon. He's cured smokers with three-pack-a-day habits in just a few sessions. Maybe you should send her to him."

Tilly waved a hand, dismissing the notion altogether. "Oh, she could never afford that."

"But you could," Finn countered. "How badly do you want her to quit?"

Tilly considered the question. "You know my luck with household staff. The second I make that investment, she'll leave us for another family." Tilly set her jaw in a firm line. "No, she'll just have to do it cold turkey."

"Good luck with that," Finn remarked.

Tilly reached out to repossess Cantaloupe just as Dean Paul bounded into the room, dragging wheeled Tumi luggage behind him.

He kissed the top of his daughter's head and gave Tilly a quick, passion-deprived peck on the lips.

"What happened?" Tilly asked, her voice full of faux alarm.

"They cut the on-set story from the budget. The next Angelina Jolie movie!" He shook his head. "This show is fucked."

"Well, I've got worse news," Tilly put in. "Veronika is still smoking!"

Dean Paul looked blankly at Tilly, then over to Finn. "Give me a few minutes to change clothes." He disappeared into the master bedroom.

Tilly watched him go. "He never pays attention to anything I say. It's ridiculous. Sometimes I think I married a twelve-year-old."

"Have you talked to Simone?" Finn asked, desperate to change the subject. He would be getting an earful from Dean Paul in a matter of moments, and he did not want to endure *Scenes from Another Troubled Lockhart Marriage* in surround sound.

Tilly sighed dramatically. "She kept me on the phone for hours last night fretting about this new girl they've added to your show. What's her name—Elsie?"

"*Emma*," Finn corrected, giving Tilly a look that let her know the amnesia act was not ready for prime time. He wanted to add, "You remember her. She's your husband's ex-girlfriend." But he resisted.

"Whatever. Anyway, Simone is a wreck, because she wants to be the only young pretty girl on set, and now she has some competition. I finally hung up on her. I had my own crisis to deal with. Maria did the midweek shopping and brought home produce that was *not* organic. She tries to get away with going to the dodgier market just to escape an extra three blocks of walking. I thought Hispanics had a stronger work ethic than that."

"Didn't she just have surgery on her hip?" Finn asked.

"A little walking is good for recovery," Tilly insisted. "That's what my trainer says, and he's also a physical therapist." She kissed Cantaloupe on the cheek with a loving smack. "It's so hard to find decent staff. Sometimes I think it'd be easier to do everything myself."

Dean Paul emerged in full workout gear and started for the stairs of the Tribeca triplex that had been a wedding gift from Tilly's parents. "I'll be back in a few hours."

"Don't forget," Tilly called out. "We have that thing to-night."

"What thing?" His tone failed to mask his annoyance.

"The sponsors dinner for the Pompe disease fund-raiser. I'm on the host committee. Remember?"

Finn waved good-bye to Tilly and rushed to catch up with Dean Paul, who had gone bounding out the door, down the sidewalk, and onward to Crunch.

"Wait up!" Finn huffed. "Jesus."

Dean Paul slowed down just enough for Finn to speed walk to his side.

"You've got problems with your job and your wife," Finn cracked. "Who would've ever thought you'd end up sharing the life of every middle-class man in America?"

"Shut up, twat." Dean Paul cracked a faint smile and marched on, saying nothing else, even as he led Finn through a brutal chest and abdominals workout.

When it was over, Dean Paul moodily stripped down to his shorts and made a beeline for the steam room, where he remained silent until an older gentleman exited, leaving them alone, at which point he announced, "It's over, dude."

Finn glanced up. "The show, the marriage, or both?"

Dean Paul sighed heavily, rearranging his body to lay flat on the tile. "For now, just the show. The numbers suck. Our main New York affiliate just switched our time slot to three o'clock in the goddamn morning."

Finn was hardly surprised. *Hollywood Live* was a syndicated infotainment program gunning for the same audience as *Entertainment Tonight*, *Access Hollywood*, *The Insider*, *Extra*, and *E! News Daily*. Every media analyst in the business had called this months ago, but Dean Paul never bothered to read the trades, so his own show's failure was breaking news to him.

Dean Paul laughed a little.

"What?" Finn wondered.

"No, it's just . . . between us, you're the one with the better job now. I never would've called that one."

"We haven't even seen our first airdate yet."

"Some success is inevitable, man."

Finn sat there basking in the wet heat, resting his tight muscles, and hoping like mad that Dean Paul was right. After all, success would mean financial independence. And for once, he needed it.

Since graduating from Brown University, he had been little more than a dilettante—a bit of sailing, a stab at modeling, a halfhearted foray into screenwriting. The trust fund from his family's real estate fortune allowed for such indulgences.

But then his parents entered some kind of late-life crisis that prompted them to save the world, or at the very least, Louisiana and Mississippi. Hurricane Katrina conjured up the inner crusading philanthropist dormant within them. The Robards not only donated mountains of money, they also flew to the most heavily damaged sites to make certain that the funds were being spent appropriately.

And then, fearing they might have raised another Hilton sister, his parents zeroed in on their social gadfly son and suddenly ordered him to work for a living. In the beginning, Finn stubbornly insisted that he was a writer. But when his father demanded to read some of his work and Finn could only produce thirty pages of a screenplay that he had been toiling over for years, it became clear to even Finn that he was not, in fact, a writer.

Luckily, *The Beehive* opportunity had come about quite organically. Finn was drunk on frozen Cosmos at G Lounge and holding court on everything from Tom Cruise to George Bush when a man slipped him a business card and said that he could make him the gay Kelly Ripa.

"If that means I get to sleep with Mark Consuelos, then I'm very interested," Finn had replied. The following morning he called Jay Lufkin, met with a series of executives over the next several days, and received an offer to join the show before he had even secured professional representation. It was funny. The entire process of landing the job had been easier than not writing a screenplay.

The steam jets hissed into action.

"Have you heard from Lara?" Dean Paul asked.

Finn nodded. "She's doing great." Lara Ward was a significant ex-girlfriend of Dean Paul's, Finn's best friend, and now happily married to a plastic surgeon in Beverly Hills, where her event planning firm, Regrets Only, was doing blockbuster business. The void of her departure had somehow fused a friendship bond between Finn and Dean Paul that continued to surprise both of them.

"She misses me, doesn't she?" Dean Paul asked.

Wearily, Finn gave him a quizzical look.

"I should've knocked it out one last time before she got married. I was her first, you know. Back in college. I popped that sweet cherry in my off-campus apartment."

Trying to remain cool, Finn betrayed no reaction. This was new ground for him—a platonic relationship with a notoriously straight guy. The possibility of it developing into anything else was nonexistent. But Dean Paul's attractiveness was difficult to ignore, and when he talked about his previous sexual exploits—which was often—Finn found himself uncomfortably turned on.

"Your name didn't even come up," Finn lied. The truth was, he and Lara had discussed Dean Paul for at least ten minutes during a twenty-minute conversation.

Dean Paul groaned. "God, I don't want to go to this fucking dinner tonight."

"It's for a good cause," Finn reasoned.

"What'd she say it was for?"

"Pompe disease."

"I don't even know what the hell that is," Dean Paul grumbled. "She drives me crazy with that shit. Even her charity diseases have to be designer."

Finn laughed. "Hey, you married her."

Dean Paul did a pantomime with his hand of a gun to the head.

"Come on, are things really that bad?"

Dean shook both hands in a comical choking gesture.

"She tries to control *everything*. Nothing matters unless she wants it to matter. And even the dumbest shit gets treated like an international incident."

"Hasn't she always been this way?" Finn asked.

"Yeah, pretty much," Dean Paul admitted. "Don't ask me why. If it wasn't for Cantaloupe . . ."

"Please. That would make two divorces. You'd be almost halfway to Billy Bob Thornton country."

Dean Paul shook his head. "She's not comfortable with me having any women friends. And she hates my guy friends." One beat. "Except you. Only because you're gay, though." He laughed. "It'd serve her right if you were sucking my cock whenever we got together."

Finn stopped breathing. He could not tell whether that was a joke or an invitation.

THE IT PARADE
BY JINX WIATT

Fill in the Blanks

Even Gucci girls fall on hard times. A certain model slash actress slash soon-to-be talk show host was in the double G boutique on Fifth Avenue attempting to buy the new top-handle bag in black patent leather. But declined credit cards (one right after another until she ran out of stock) prevented her from closing the deal. The Nubian princess left in tears. Here's hoping her new employer offers a pay advance. She needs all the retail therapy she can get on account of that psycho ex-boyfriend, who just happens to be baseball's hottest outfield attraction.

4

Simone

It was like being in one of those big budget, loud Hollywood disaster movies. As the world fell down all around her, Simone Williams was running as fast as she could.

She burst inside her sunny one-bedroom Upper East Side apartment and flattened her back against the door, chest heaving.

The humiliation was total—possibly her most embarrassing moment ever. Worse than the flat-on-her-face fall she took on the Paris runway during her first Karl Lagerfeld show. Even worse than the time she vomited on William L. Petersen when she guest-starred on *CSI: Crime Scene Investigation*.

Oh, God, yes, this situation was far worse. Being denied credit on Fifth Avenue. Over and over again.

Chanel, a beautiful silver Egyptian Mau, chortled a soft melody, delighted by Simone's return. The feline wiggled her tail at great speed as she treaded the hardwood floor with her forepaws.

Simone made a direct move for the antique rolltop desk, lifting it up to reveal a disaster underneath. She fired up her sleek new black MacBook and sorted through piles of statements and scribbled Post-its in a mad search for user names, passwords, and account numbers.

With a steadily rising panic, she logged on to check her balances, card by card. American Express Optima, American Express Blue, Citi Platinum Visa, MBNA Platinum MasterCard, Capital One Visa, and so on. Every account had careened past its approved credit line.

For a moment, Simone struggled to breathe. This was impossible. How could every credit card be maxed out? An internal thunderbolt dropped. Somebody must have stolen her identity!

She retraced her online steps to check recent activity. Hmm. All of the charges looked very much like her own—the same restaurants, retail boutiques, and beauty outlets that Simone had frequented over the last week glowed back on the thirteen-inch monitor.

For at least two hours, she worked the phone, enduring interminable holding spells for account managers and supervisors in an all-out bid to have her credit lines increased. Most of them hovered around twenty thousand. Maybe that was an acceptable limit for a college student. But Simone Williams was hardly a struggling coed.

Not long ago she had been featured in the *Us Weekly* "Who Wore It Best?" contest (against Jessica Simpson). They were both pictured in the same Cavalli black paisley-print empire-waist dress. Of course, Jessica had won with seventy-two percent of the votes. But only because she was more famous and had bigger boobs. Anyway, the point of the Cingular Wireless assault was to boost Simone's credit lines to a level commensurate with her celebrity potential.

But not a single request was granted. Apparently, the worst time to ask for an increase was when you were already over the original credit limit. Simone's frustration was total. On the final attempt with the last card, she called the American Express representative an ugly cow before hanging up.

Chanel was stretched out in grossly indulgent lazy cat slumber. Somewhere beneath her lay the calculator that could add up the debt damage. But why disturb Chanel for such a depressing task? It could be done later. Anyway, Simone knew the ballpark figure was around two hundred thousand—on her revolving credit cards. There were American Express Gold and Platinum accounts totaling about fifty thousand that the company expected to be paid in full.

She stared at the messy stack of suffocating bills and let out a groan. If only. If only there had been just enough room left for that Gucci bag. The one with the medium top-handle in black patent leather with zip-pocket detail, goldtone GG hardware, and detachable shoulder strap. Yes. If only that purchase had gone through, then Simone would be content and able to deal with this crisis like a true princess warrior.

She left the financial crime scene and poured herself some Chardonnay. Followed by another. Wine could be a brilliant problem solver. By the end of a third glass, she usually had answers for all the squabbles in the Middle East, not to mention ways Alec Baldwin and Kim Basinger could get along.

Money. So yummy. So yucky, too. It had definitely been a glorious solution and epic problem over the years, simultaneously providing her great comfort and total destruction. She stroked Chanel's smooth, spotted coat, feeling the impact of the wine as the memories bubbled to the surface.

Simone grew up with money. Plenty of it. Her father had been a corporate executive, her mother a Junior League dynamo. Their only child possessed toffee-colored skin, emerald green eyes, straight hair, and a tall, lithe frame. By the time she turned three, Simone knew she was gorgeous. Everybody gushed about it, and even at that age, she had to agree with them.

In the cosseted enclaves of Atlanta's Buckhead area, Simone had basked in a privileged, preppy environment, thinking of herself more as an individual than as a member of any particular race. The pro-black mind-set completely escaped her. Yes, Martin Luther King Jr. had a dream. But Diana Vreeland, the legendary fashion editor for *Harper's Bazaar*, had epic style.

When Simone read that DV had once declared pink the navy blue of India, she considered it a vastly underreported moment in cultural study, wrote a paper on the subject for her world history class, and turned in the manifesto on pink paper. Mrs. Boozer gave her an F. That was the day Simone decided to be a model. She was twelve.

By thirteen, she was a professional poser, already the perfect sample size and modeling for catalogs and upscale retail trunk shows, in addition to commercial work, some of it national, like the Sprite television ad that had her dancing in the street with wild abandon. At fifteen, Simone was already living overseas without her parents.

DV had once proclaimed, "the best thing about London is Paris." And she was, as always, spot on. Simone adored France. It was a fast lane life of go-sees, runway work, champagne and cigarettes, and modelizers on the make. By sixteen, she had made herself available as the mistress of a rich married man (for great gifts) and the girlfriend of a hot young club promoter (for great fun).

But at seventeen, she was back in Atlanta, no longer a fresh face for the Paris agencies and having offended Karl Lagerfeld by pulling a no-show at a dinner party in his honor. At the time, she had been kidnapped by her married lover, who was coked out of his mind and paranoid that she was cheating on him with his nephew. As it turns out, the club promoter *was* his nephew. Really, though, how could she have known? It seemed like everybody in France had the same last name.

Simone's homecoming was fraught with rude awakenings. In her absence, the company that her father worked for had imploded in financial scandal, wiping out retirement accounts and inciting a federal inquiry that buried top executives, including her father, in legal bills. Without Simone's permission, her parents raided her savings, depleting every dollar she had ever earned. And yet they still lost the house and were forced to move into an apartment.

Ultimately, the stress and humiliation proved too much for her father. He died of a heart attack at the age of forty-six. Her mother moved into a smaller rental unit and accepted a job behind the Guerlain cosmetics counter at Neiman Marcus. And Simone moved to New York with less than a thousand dollars to her name.

The stateside modeling opportunities turned out to be middling at best, and playing agency hopscotch did nothing to improve the situation. It was infuriating to settle for department store catalog work while Queen Latifah signed on with CoverGirl for millions. Where was the justice?

On a lark, Simone had signed up for a one-day acting class taught by Pamela Anderson at The Learning Annex. It was two hours well spent. With her new thespian skills she vaulted into acting and got lucky with a semi-regular series of one-off guest shots on episodic TV shows, most of them hour-long procedural dramas of the *Law and Order* variety. Usually, she got selected for uppity model or junior society type parts. Casting agents did not see her as the gritty prostitute, the stone-faced government worker, or the around-the-way girl with an out-of-wedlock child by an NBA star, which accounted for ninety-nine percent of available roles for black actresses.

For the past few years, Simone had been cobbling together income from random modeling assignments and bit player acting jobs, subsidizing cash, lifestyle, and clothing needs with credit card accounts that seemed to grow like sea monkeys.

An envelope emblazoned with the words YOU ARE APPROVED seemed to arrive in her mailbox at least every other day. It had actually been good for her self-esteem. On a morning when you got passed over for Burn Victim Number Two on *Rescue Me*, sometimes a girl needed a pair of Christian Louboutin platform Mary Janes in red leather, even if they did cost seven hundred dollars.

Simone's cellular hummed to life to the tune of *I Dream of Jeannie*. Cautiously, she checked the ID screen, saw TILLY CALLING, and felt a moment's relief, followed by a frisson of irritation.

Tilly was arguably her closest friend, but sometimes Simone struggled to get past the fact that Tilly came from a wealthy family (that managed to hold on to their fortune), married a rich husband (who was also gorgeous), had been blessed with a gorgeous baby (with no stretch marks to show for it, thanks to obsessive slathering of belly balm by Biggs and Featherbelle), *and* earned a mint as an endorsement model for 24/7 Cosmetics, a job that required ten days of work per year at the most, five of which (all in-store appearances) Tilly refused to show up for because she hated to shake hands with strangers. It was not just an embarrassment of riches. It was obscene.

"Hi, Tilly," Simone half-sang, half-sighed.

"We just got back from Starbucks and barely escaped with our lives. Some horrible woman touched Cantaloupe's face with her icky fingers. She seemed like the sweet grandmother type, but she could've just as easily been a terrorist.

I've already given Cantaloupe a bath. It's her third one today already. I feel like I've been assaulted." She breathed a dramatic sigh. "How are *you*?"

"Not so good. I was sitting here—"

"Dean Paul's show is about to be cancelled any minute," Tilly cut in. "Which means I'm now the major breadwinner for this family. As if I need any additional pressure! Thank God my parents bought us this apartment. Otherwise, I don't know what we'd do. Cantaloupe needs stability at this age. I couldn't bear a move right now. Are you nervous about tomorrow?"

Simone had scarcely thought about it. Her first official day to report to the set of *The Beehive*. All she really cared about was the regular income and the chance that maybe— just maybe—it would lead to some kind of lucrative long-term spokesmodel gig, even if it was with a budget retailer like Kohl's that merchandised apparel in large sizes. "I haven't really thought about it until now."

"Promise that you'll call and tell me *everything*," Tilly insisted. "I want to know what she looks like without makeup. My guess is that she has bad skin like Cameron Diaz."

Simone rolled her eyes skyward and refilled her Chardonnay. *She* was Emma Ronson, Dean Paul's most recent ex. As always, Tilly's inquiry about Simone's life really had everything to do with Tilly.

BEEP. The sound was precisely the exit opportunity that Simone needed. "Someone's calling on the other line."

"Oh, well, I can't talk anyway. It's time for Cantaloupe's Japanese language lesson."

Simone tensed at the sight of UNKNOWN CALLER on her cellular display. She hesitated, then realized that it could be one of her credit card companies calling back with a change of heart, so she answered abruptly. "Hello?"

There was no response. But in the background she heard what sounded like bar noise.

"Hello?"

Still nothing. Finally, the line went dead.

Tears sprang to Simone's eyes as she slammed the phone shut. "Crazy son of a bitch!"

It did not matter that she had changed her number six times in as many months. He always found a way to get to her.

Damn Tommy Robb. Damn him to hell!

THE IT PARADE
BY JINX WIATT

Fill in the Blanks

And you thought *The View* once had its share of dysfunctions. No set is in need of an on-the-premises therapist quite like that new show generating oodles of honey buzz. One cohost was recently dumped by her ex. That ex is now dating another cohost, who is still smarting from her breakup with America's prince. Another cohost is the new BFF of America's prince. And still another cohost is BFF to America's prince's new wife. Got it? If not, start from the top and read again.

5

Sutton

Three soft knocks rapped the dressing room door.

"What is it?" Sutton snapped.

Jay Lufkin poked his head inside. "They need you in hair and makeup."

Sutton glared at him. "Have them come to me. I'm not sitting in the same room with her."

Jay sighed. "You're about to share a set with—"

"That's something I *have* to do," Sutton cut in. "Don't get the two issues confused. Tell Joey and Olivia I'm ready whenever they are." She turned her attention to the background material for today's guests. "Are you serious about these Japanese twins?"

"Faith Hill has a sinus infection," Jay explained. "This is an eleventh-hour save."

Sutton gave him a withering look.

"Okay, *save* may not be the right word. But 'Bee in Our Bonnet' is already running for two segments. We need them."

"Good-bye, Jay," Sutton sang dismissively without so much as a glance upward.

Mio and Mako Kometani were the identical twin daughters of a billionaire industrialist father and celebrated in their country of origin for being crowned Miss Japan (Mio one year, Mako the very next) and successfully marketing a line of products ranging from noodles to bust cream. Now their desperate bid for stateside, Paris Hilton–like fame was catching on with a hit reality series on the Oxygen network called *Deep Inside M&M*.

Last night Sutton had attempted to screen an entire hour-long episode but gave up after the first thirty minutes, which chronicled Mio and Mako's bikini wax appointment and their attempts to change the outgoing voice mail messages on their cell phones. When Sutton saw that the remainder of the show would feature the twins doing little more than counting the shoes in their closets and fighting over a D&G dress, she promptly powered down the DVD player.

Sutton's stomach did a complete revolution as a realization became clear. A few months ago she had been grilling Condoleezza Rice about Iran's nuclear capabilities. Today she would be lobbing questions to Mio and Mako about the number of shoes in their closet.

Just as the door to her dressing room opened, Sutton heard Jay cry out from the corridor, "No! Not that room!"

But it was too late. In front of her stood a confused delivery boy holding an explosion of mango and burgundy calla lilies in an antique silver vase. The arrangement was from Ariston Florist on Fifth Avenue. Sutton instantly recognized the meticulous work of owner Thomas Barbagianis. Garrison kept the Greek-born florist on speed dial. For one stupid, vulnerable moment, Sutton's heart lifted with emotion. Was he wishing her good luck on what would be her first show? Maybe he . . .

Suddenly, the sight of Jay's pained expression triggered the intellectual truth that Sutton already knew. The flowers were not for her. Garrison had sent them to that bitch.

Sutton betrayed nothing as Jay quietly ushered the delivery person out of the room and down the hall, returning moments later with an effusive apology.

She halted him. "It's okay, Jay." Then she gestured to her packet of research. "I need to see someone about the graphics for the 'Bee in Our Bonnet' segment. Would that be Candace?"

Jay nodded, searching Sutton's eyes for more. "What about the graphics?"

"I just want to go over the image sequence and make sure we're in synch." She smiled at him. "Jay, I hope you have more pressing matters than intercepting flower deliveries and micromanaging the work of a production assistant. Otherwise, this show is in trouble."

Jay conceded her point with a sigh. "Be nice to Candace. I don't need her to quit. She's too good."

Sutton drew back dramatically. "Am I some kind of monster?"

"You made the set designer cry," Jay pointed out.

Sutton shrugged. "Allowing Sarah to go on thinking she's talented is ultimately a disservice. I care about her."

"Well, in that case, when it comes to Candace, try to be as unfeeling as possible." Jay rolled his eyes, darting out of the way as the hair and makeup team bounded inside Sutton's sanctuary.

"Okay, Queen Bee," Joey intoned breathlessly. "Let's make you the most fabulous of all." He positioned himself behind her and began finger-styling her hair, studying the results through the dressing mirror. "Nervous?"

"Amateurs get nervous," Sutton informed him grandly.

Joey, his tanned, toned, tattooed body packed into a tight T-shirt, shared a secret smile with Olivia, the plump makeup girl with unbelievably gorgeous skin.

Sutton smiled. "I take that look to mean the others are absolutely terrified."

"Maybe a few pre-show jitters," Joey murmured. "I wouldn't say they were *terrified*."

Sutton ran a hand along the wisps of hair tapering her neck. "I'm thinking of letting it grow out." Through the mirror, she searched Joey's eyes for approval.

He seemed to be considering her announcement when Olivia squealed, "Are you going to tell her, or should I?"

Sutton merely waited for the nugget to drop. Hair and makeup people could give the CIA lessons in sensitive intelligence gathering.

"A bill collector called Simone," Joey offered. "Isn't that tragic? She tried to play it off, but it was *so* obvious."

"I don't get it," Olivia put in, sorting through her Trish McEvoy brushes. "Her last boyfriend was playing for the Yankees on an eighty million dollar contract, and this girl can't make a minimum payment on her Visa bill."

"*Tommy Robb*," Joey said dreamily. "Honey, that man is welcome in my dugout anytime."

Olivia cackled.

Sutton managed a tight smile just as Candace stepped inside.

"Jay said you wanted to see me," the production assistant said.

"Oh, yes," Sutton replied, innocently enough. "Find that photograph that just hit the wire of Dean Paul Lockhart on the beach with his daughter. I'd like to lead with that in the 'Bee in Our Bonnet' segment."

Joey and Olivia traded meaningful looks.

Sutton cut an annoyed glance to Candace, who just stood there like a *Deal or No Deal* girl. "Don't let me keep you from your work, dear."

Candace quietly slunk away.

"Ooh, the devil wears St. John," Joey purred.

"Did you see her face when Finn mentioned his name this morning?" Olivia asked.

Sutton quickly surmised that Emma Ronson and Dean Paul Lockhart were the objects of Olivia's pronouns.

"Oh, so that red on her cheeks was *natural* blush," Joey cracked.

Olivia giggled. "I know the girl who did Tilly Lockhart's makeup for the last 24/7 shoot, and according to her, Tilly and Dean haven't had sex in over a month. She's on Lexapro, and it takes her forever to orgasm, so she just doesn't bother."

"Maybe he's getting it from the other side of the equator," Joey mused. "That would explain his close friendship with Finn. And it's so obvious that our token gay has the biggest crush. How many times did he name drop Dean Paul this morning?"

"Oh, I don't know . . . *fifty*?" Olivia snickered.

Joey placed both hands on Sutton's shoulders. "I hope you know that we would *never* talk about you this way," he said earnestly.

Sutton raised a perfectly waxed brow. "I believe that like I believe you've never had a cock in your mouth."

Joey and Olivia gasped in shock, then roared in laughter.

Sutton just smiled. For the moment, she was feeling no pain. But she was damn sure getting ready to cause some.

THE IT PARADE
BY JINX WIATT

Fill in the Blanks

It was the bitch slap heard all around the world on that buzz-worthy new gabfest when one of the baby bees gave the Queen Bee quite a stinger live on the air. *Ouch*. Pass the Benadryl. And we're only one show down, darlings. Spies say that Big Bad Mama wants her cheeky young cohost ousted immediately. But producers love the friction and the hot gossip being generated. So for now, nobody's going anywhere.

6

Emma

"Ninety seconds, Ms. Ronson!"

The announcement triggered a frisson of nervous energy. This was it. Do or die. Emma took in a deep breath and left the safety of her dressing room to queue up with her cohosts in the backstage holding area.

Sutton Lancaster continued to freeze her out.

Finn Robards smiled supportively and gave her hand a gentle squeeze.

Simone Williams spent the last minute staring into a jeweled compact mirror, perfecting already perfect lips.

The excitement of the studio audience was palpable. A pre-show stand-up comedian had whipped up party vibrations, and the free juice and cookies had the crowd on the crescendo of a sugar rush.

Emma braced herself for impact as the German techno-inspired theme music commenced, followed by the announcer's booming voice.

"Ladies and gentlemen, you have officially entered *The Beehive*! Please welcome your hosts . . . Sutton Lancaster . . . Emma Ronson . . . Simone Williams . . . and Finn Robards!"

Enthusiastic applause greeted Emma as she emerged from

backstage, clutching a printout of the show's breakdown like a security blanket. Heart racing, she stiffly took her place next to Sutton at the black BeeBoard table and clapped gleefully as Simone and Finn slid in to her left.

"It's our first show!" Sutton exclaimed to no one in particular. "Can you believe it?"

The audience thundered its approval.

"And for those of you who might have wandered into the wrong studio," Finn interjected saucily, "this is *The Beehive* and not *Maury*. But we'll be offering free paternity tests later in the show, so there's no need to rush off."

The studio erupted with laughter.

Emma beamed a look to Jay Lufkin. He was adorned with headset microphone gear and sat perched on the edge of his seat on the front row, flashing Finn a thumb's up sign.

Instantly, Emma picked up on the manner in which Sutton's spine straightened at the audience's enthusiastic reaction to Finn.

"This is our first broadcast," Sutton began, assuming the lead as Queen Bee. "So I think some introductions are in order. I'm Sutton Lancaster. Some of you might recognize me from various capacities on news networks, most recently Fox. To my left is Emma Ronson, former news reader for Manhattan's own News Channel Four."

Emma sat there, silently seething. *Former news reader?* She was the goddamn coanchor of the top-rated *Today in New York*!

"To Emma's left is the lovely Simone Williams," Sutton went on. "She's done a bit of modeling and acting here and there. And finally we have Finn Robards." She laughed a little. "Now Finn, other than being handsome and funny, I'm not sure what is it that you've done to earn your place here."

"Isn't that enough?" Finn cracked. "After all, this *is* morning television."

Once again, the audience whooped with laughter.

Emma watched as Sutton managed a humorous smile through grinding teeth.

"More importantly, this is *The Beehive*," Sutton continued. "And every beehive has a queen bee. Taking into account my . . . *ahem* . . . maturity and experience, I suppose that would be me."

"Now wait a minute," Finn cut in with faux outrage. "I thought *I* was the queen bee?" One beat. "Or am I just the queen?"

The audience roared with laughter.

Emma stepped into the fray to assert her position. "I'm glad our audience is in good spirits, because we have some disappointing news. Faith Hill was scheduled to join us today, but she's been sidelined with a sinus infection."

A chorus of moans echoed from the crowd.

"But Faith has promised to reschedule," Emma went on brightly. "And today we're lucky to have reality sensations Mio and Mako Kometani from the hit series *Deep Inside M&M*."

The audience clapped with genuine enthusiasm, surprisingly mollified.

"Okay, I'm totally obsessed with that show," Simone put in. "I can't stop watching it. You know the episode where they count all the shoes in their closet? I've watched it, like, three times. I'm totally into shoes, so that part was, like, porn to me."

"Did you masturbate to it?" Finn asked.

Simone drew in a shocked breath. "No!"

The crowd went ballistic.

"Well, *you* brought up the porn analogy," Finn remarked.

Emma started to break in but could not stop laughing.

Finn, obviously delighted with the response and completely in his element, muttered, "I'll be here all week."

"Now there's much more on today's show than twin sisters who shop," Sutton interjected, cutting Finn a scolding glance. "Family therapist Dr. Sallie Payne will be here to tell us about the disturbing rise of clinical depression among teenage girls. We'll have a South Beach Diet cooking class with the Food Network's very own Jessie Ciccone, and we're going to learn how to burn belly fat with an abdominals workout that takes just *five* minutes a day. Fitness guru Gail Terrell will be here to take us through it. But before all of that, we're going to launch our very first 'Bee in Our Bonnet' segment. This is our chance to buzz around the table on topics that viewers are talking about at home. Let's get started on a subject that seems to be fascinating the country more and more . . . *celebrity babies*."

Sutton gestured an open hand toward the audience. "How many of you went absolutely gaga over Shiloh Jolie-Pitt and Suri Cruise?"

The applause that came thundering back indicated that many of those in attendance indeed had.

"And what about *this* famous bundle of joy?" Sutton asked, shifting in her seat to glance back at the mega-screen behind her.

The audience practically swooned.

Emma turned to see a JumboTron-like display of Dean Paul Lockhart with baby Cantaloupe on the beach, the same image that had nearly upended her just a day earlier. She could feel a wave of heat rise up from her neck to her face.

"Thank God the child is gorgeous," Finn said. "With a name like Cantaloupe, she's going to need every possible advantage in the world."

A chorus of titters swept through the crowd.

"She definitely has her father's mouth," Sutton observed. "And his eyes, too. Don't you agree, Emma?"

Emma looked at Sutton, momentarily taken aback by the venom spewing from the veteran journalist's gaze. "She's a beautiful child."

"How could she not be?" Sutton fawned. "Coming from that gene pool—a dreamboat father and a mother who's a stunning beauty. Those two met, married, and became parents so quickly. It must've been love at first sight."

Emma felt the fire of rapidly rising blood. The bitch had gone too far. If Sutton Lancaster wanted to fight dirty, then Emma Ronson was more than capable of getting down in the muck. "I wouldn't know. Since I'm involved in a relationship of my own, I don't really take the time to speculate on other people's."

Sutton's face registered the hit. "I just think it's an interesting phenomenon—this celebrity baby craze," she mused silkily. "In a case such as this, perhaps the real interest is the fantasy of having a child with a man like Dean Paul Lockhart."

"For some women maybe," Emma replied, making the decision to move in for the kill, if only to prove that she was not to be fucked with. "For other women, say, those past childbearing years, it could be the regret of never having had children and facing the remainder of their life alone."

Sutton's eyes blazed hatred.

"Simone, I'm afraid we're sharing the stage with two silly, overanalytical bitches," Finn chided. "Sometimes a rose is just a rose. People like cute babies! Am I right?" He shouted the question to the audience.

The booming ovation provided the answer.

"You couldn't be more right," Simone added. "People like celebrity babies, because so many regular ones are just plain ugly."

A low rumble percolated through the audience.

Immediately, Emma could sense them turning on Simone.

"I know that's mean to say," Simone went on dangerously. "But everyone in this studio knows that there are some ugly babies out there. I mean, we've all seen them, right? So when a Cantaloupe Lockhart comes along, we're basically *grateful*. Everybody loves pretty things."

"I'm going to go out on a limb here and declare this woman more shallow than Paris Hilton," Finn announced. "And I say that with the utmost respect. I think she's brilliant."

The audience applauded its approval.

"Stay with us after the break," Finn continued, taking a cue from Jay. "Because we're coming right back with more bees in our bonnet."

Emma waited for the theme music to subside before storming off the set, fighting off tears with each step. She could not do this. The fight was simply not in her to wage battle on the air day in and day out.

"Emma, wait," Jay called out.

She spun on him angrily. "I'm sorry, Jay. I can't do this."

"You're already doing it," Jay praised. "Sutton went after you with her claws out, and you got some serious licks in."

Emma shook her head. "I'm not proud of that."

"You should be. It's going to make you a daytime star."

THE IT PARADE
BY *JINX WIATT*

Fill in the Blanks

A straight guy best friend. It's the must-have accessory for every *swish* boat veteran in Manhattan. Trust me, darlings. By comparison, the new Prada collection is an afterthought. And television's newest gay sensation (those *Queer Eye* lads are beyond over) has bagged what may be the premium hetero pal in America's prince. But with all the whispers about this pseudo-royal's lackluster sex life with the new wife (babies can be quite the libido killer), one has to wonder. Is this MWM just an open-minded fag stag, or is he part of the ever-growing legion of the bi-curious?

7

Finn

"I don't know what any of it means," Finn said, staring down at the scribble scratched onto the back of a Barney's receipt.

Dean Paul made a face. "Don't look at me. All that ratings shit gives me a headache."

Tilly sighed her annoyance. "The two of you have no business acumen whatsoever." She snatched the perplexing note from Finn's side of the table. "You're like two dumb jocks."

Finn beamed. "No one's ever called me a jock before."

"You're more like a dumb cheerleader," Dean Paul corrected. "I'm the dumb jock."

Finn just sat there, momentarily deflated. Dean Paul had a cruel habit of always pointing out who was the real man and who was the faggot.

"These are one-day metered results from fifty-five markets," Tilly began. "*The Beehive* improved on its lead-in by double digits. The same goes for year-ago time period averages. Wow." She looked up at Finn. "It's not just good news. It's *great* news."

"Assuming viewers will watch again," Dean Paul put in.

Tilly slapped her husband's shoulder. "Stop being a jerk. Just because *your* show is tanking . . ."

"Hey, I don't care," Dean Paul said defiantly, proof that he *did* care, a great deal, in fact. "Maybe I'll become a househusband. You're always threatening to fire Veronika. Now's your chance."

Tilly raised her hands in faux horror. "I can't even trust you to change Cantaloupe's diaper."

Finn laughed. "Are you that pathetic?"

"Hell, no!" Dean Paul protested, instantly offended. He looked at Tilly accusingly. "I know how to change a diaper."

"You don't wipe her properly, and she ends up with a nasty rash whenever you change her. Househusbandry is *not* for you." Tilly checked her watch. "Sorry, boys. I have to go. I have an interview with a personal shopper in thirty minutes. She's supposed to be the best, and she only has one client opening."

Finn registered surprise. "I can't believe that *you* would ever outsource shopping." He laughed a little. "I guess motherhood has changed you."

"Oh, it's not for me," Tilly clarified. "This shopper is for Cantaloupe."

Dean Paul turned toward his wife in disbelief. When he spoke, his voice was flat. "The personal shopper is for Cantaloupe." One beat. "Our six-month-old baby."

"Children's couture sells out in a flash, and I don't have time to go store to store trying to find the right size. These last few months have been a nightmare." Abruptly, Tilly slid out of the booth and stood up. "Finn, congratulations. The show's a hit. Darling, I'll see you at home. Cross your fingers for this shopper to agree to take Cantaloupe on." With a fluttery wave, Tilly dashed out of Balthazar.

Dean Paul looked at Finn. "I don't know about you, but I plan on getting drunk." He flagged down the waitress to order another bottle of wine.

"Are you really that surprised?" Finn asked. "I mean, this is the same woman who hired a sleep consultant from Switzerland to stop Cantaloupe from crying at night."

Wearily, Dean Paul shook his head and drained what remained in Tilly's wineglass. It was the only alcohol within reach. "I don't get her, man. She obsesses over the kid, but she outsources everything."

Finn often wondered why Dean Paul found anything about Tilly surprising. A few minutes with her generally told the whole story. So in answer, he just raised his brow and waited for the my-fucking-wife moment to pass. "Did you watch yesterday's show? You never said."

"Yeah, I did." He glanced up, a smirk on his face, knowingly withholding the approval that he obviously knew Finn craved.

"*Well?*"

Dean Paul shrugged. "It's a chick show," he said dismissively. "The estrogen level is radioactive."

Finn's spirits sank.

"But you were good. In fact, I'd say you were *The Beehive's* secret weapon."

Finn's spirits soared again. "Really?"

Dean Paul nodded fast, ready to move on. "What's up with those Japanese twins?"

Finn laughed. "Mio and Mako? How did you like their performance of Mary J. Blige's 'No More Drama'?"

"I only listened to the first few bars before muting the sound. Then I just watched and fantasized about nailing both of them at the same time."

The waitress returned and went through the ceremony of opening the new bottle.

Dean Paul took quick possession and filled up two glasses. "I've never had a three-way. Can you believe that? No three-ways, no guys . . . I guess I haven't lived."

Finn stirred slightly in his seat, not quite sure whether he should respond or not.

Thankfully, Dean Paul saved him the trouble. "How long can that show go on before Emma and Sutton get into a serious catfight?"

"I'm surprised we got through the first day without one. I felt sorry for Emma, though. When that image of you and Cantaloupe flashed, her face looked pretty raw."

Dean Paul drank deep on his wine.

"What happened with the two of you anyway?" Finn asked.

"Nothing, really. Typical relationship stuff. She was pushing for a real commitment. She wanted kids. I just wasn't ready."

Finn leveled a serious look at Dean Paul. "But you married Tilly less than a year after you broke up with Emma. And the two of you had a baby right away."

"So?"

"*So* . . . from Emma's vantage point, those would be some tough facts to get over."

Dean Paul tilted his head and raised his glass. "Not my problem."

Finn regarded him curiously. "What did your mother do to you as a child?"

He smiled at the insinuation. "Nothing traumatic, Dr. Phil. I've just always been able to get away with shit when it comes to girls. Back in high school, I would date a girl for about three months, get what I wanted, and then pretend like I didn't know her when I showed up at a party with a new chick."

"And you're proud of this?" Finn challenged.

"No, but it didn't stop girls from dating me. They knew what the deal was."

Finn took a generous sip of wine. "So explain this, super stud. How is it that you let women like Lara and Emma slip away and end up marrying the Aspens and the Tillys of the world?"

Dean Paul groaned miserably. "Oh, shit. I can't believe you just pulled the Aspen card. That's cold."

Finn laughed.

Aspen Bauer's claim to fame was a stint on MTV's *The Real World*. Her marriage to Dean Paul lasted only a few months, after which she served jail time for fleeing the scene of a hit-and-run accident that left a child in a coma.

"The last thing I heard about her was that she was doing that pay-per-view Lingerie Bowl on Super Bowl Sunday." Dean Paul shook his head. "I can't believe I married her. What was I thinking?"

His attention faltered as a model-thin brunette sashayed past the booth. Dean Paul tracked her with a heat-seeking gaze until she was out of sight.

"Do you know her?"

"I'd like to. I bet she tastes good in all the right places." He laughed and refilled his wine.

"Would you ever cheat on Tilly?" Finn wondered.

"She takes Lexapro. The drive is still there, but it takes her forever to come, so she doesn't want to be bothered most of the time. We're a once-a-month couple at best."

"Is that a yes?" Finn asked.

"How long could *you* live on boring sex once a month?" Dean Paul countered.

"I don't know. Probably longer than you."

"Are you seeing anyone that I don't know about?"

Finn could feel his face grow hot. Whenever Dean Paul inquired about his dating life, he became instantly uncomfortable. "Not really."

"*Not really?* Guess you're still hanging out in the back rooms of clubs late at night."

"I've never done that!" Finn protested angrily.

Dean Paul zeroed in with a ray-gun gaze. "*Never?*"

"Well . . . it's been years," Finn admitted.

"Whore." Dean Paul drank up and laughed.

Finn glanced around the restaurant. It was past two o'clock, and the lunch rush had filtered out, leaving Balthazar, the French bistro on SoHo's Spring Street, which was usually crammed to capacity, refreshingly near empty. "You never answered my question."

"I'm almost hammered. Refresh my memory."

"Would you ever cheat on Tilly?"

Dean Paul gave Finn a tipsy stare. "You're assuming I haven't already."

Finn rolled his eyes. "Stupid me."

"I was in L.A. for *Hollywood Live* last May working the upfronts for the new television season. There was this hot young actress who's on some CW sitcom that'll probably be cancelled next week. I hit it. Couldn't resist. But that's the only time. Are you ashamed of me?"

Finn raised up both hands in mock surrender. "No judgment here. It's your life."

"This is just between us, right? If you tell any of those bitches on that show, it'll get to Simone and then back to Tilly."

"I know how to keep a confidence."

"Good. And don't be jealous. Who knows? Next time I cheat, maybe it'll be with you."

THE IT PARADE
BY JINX WIATT

Fill in the Blanks

And you thought Kimora Lee Simmons was a vacuous glamazon in grave need of a tour of hunger-ravaged Africa. Some say Kimora has the empathy of Angelina Jolie when compared to the latest shallow princess on the scene. As she wrapped up her first week on that new morning gabfest—a surprise runaway hit—station e-mail boxes were cyber-stuffed with complaints from parents of less-than-beautiful babies, overweight people, Christians, lesbians with bad haircuts, women with more than one cat, and men named Chad. Who will she offend next week?

8

Simone

Simone glanced down at the Christian Dior handbag, then back to her reflection in the boutique's full-length mirror. The aged leather and suede messenger hobo looked good on her. *Very good.*

"I don't know how Punch secured one of these for you without prepayment. This is a wait-listed item, and we're sold out for the season. I can't hold it beyond today."

"In other words, you're saying, 'Decide now, bitch,' " Simone murmured, spinning to survey her most flattering side.

Alexandra, a commission-hungry sales barracuda, pursed her collagen-treated lips. "In a manner of speaking."

Lovingly, Simone fingered the handbag's gorgeous hardware. Punch always offered up some sort of discount, but she was off on this particular day. What horrible luck.

Simone adored Punch. She was sophisticated and bubbly. They had bonded over the shared misfortune of having been involved with professional baseball stars. Hard lesson learned: Any eighteen-year-old man who skips college and heads straight into the dugout with a contract for mega-millions in his back pocket should be staunchly avoided.

Alexandra gave a tight little smile of impatience.

Inspecting the purse, Simone stalled for time, her brain computer running the disturbing calculations. Her first salary installment from *The Beehive* had only managed to stop the financial bleeding momentarily.

All the debts just sucked up cash like a Hoover Dirt Devil. After paying the mortgage, second mortgage, consolidation loan, building maintenance, utilities, and daily living expenses, Simone found herself broke all over again. But this Dior purse was only fifteen hundred dollars. Considering her current state of affairs, adding that to the pile would hardly make a difference.

She fished into her wallet and grabbed the first piece of plastic her fingers could connect with. "I'll take it."

"The lady's got good taste."

Simone cut her gaze to the man who was suddenly invading her personal space. Unimpressed, she turned away.

"Hi, Ke*von*," Alexandra gushed. "I'll be with you in a flash. I'm just wrapping things up here."

"I'll take one of those, too." He reached out to stroke the handbag with a manicured, diamond-studded hand.

Reflexively, Simone drew back.

"Hey, don't freak, Foxy Brown. I ain't moving in on your shit."

Simone was appalled. This man had just called her *Foxy Brown* and cursed at her in public!

"Wrap one up for me, baby." Now he was addressing Alexandra. "I need a little happy to quiet a bitch down. You know what I'm saying?"

Simone secretly wanted to call 911. This pig should be arrested.

A pained expression skated across Alexandra's face. "Kevon, I'm *so* sorry. We are completely sold out of this bag." She cut an accusing glance in Simone's direction. "This is our last one in the store."

The man reached into the front pocket of his baggy warm-up pants and pulled out a bulging wad of crisp one hundred dollar bills. "How much you want for it, shorty?"

Simone could hardly believe the situation. Who *was* this vulgar beast?

He started to peel off the cash at a rapid clip, sometimes moving two or three at a time. "Just tell me when to stop."

Simone regarded him like a derelict on the sidewalk. He was black, muscled, outfitted in a white velvet tracksuit and high-top sneakers, and dripping in garish diamonds, including an enormous dollar sign pendant as large as a door knocker.

After a moment, Simone turned away in disgust and pushed the Dior treasure into Alexandra's spindle-thin arms. "Would you please just ring this up?"

The shop girl shrugged diffidently and disappeared into the back.

Without warning, bass-heavy hip-hop music screamed into the air. "All my bitches eating up my cell phone minutes/Every day and all night/These hos just eating up my cell phone minutes . . ."

Simone realized with a current of outrage that this misogynistic aural assault was the thug's mobile ring tone.

"Yo! Just chilling, motherfucker. Crept up in Dior to get a little something-something for one of my dick divers. You know how it is."

In a huff, Simone stalked away, intercepting Alexandra just as she returned.

With a cold glare, she slapped Simone's American Express Platinum onto the counter and rudely slid it back in her direction. "Your card was declined."

"There must be some mistake," Simone said automatically. It was her rote response to this all too common embarrassment of late.

"I ran it through twice." Alexandra sighed. "Do you have another form of payment?"

Simone could feel a flush of heat spread up from her neck. Nervously, she ransacked her purse and snatched out what looked to be half a dozen cards. "I'm having a problem with my bank. Just keep trying until one works."

She stood there for what seemed like forever, nervously drumming her fingers on the counter until Alexandra returned, this time with a receipt, the sight of which triggered a grateful sigh of relief.

"All of these were declined as well," Alexandra pointed out, handing over five credit cards. "This is the one that was charged." She slammed down a gold Visa.

Simone shot back a haughty glare as she scribbled her signature. "I can't believe you let people like *him* in this store. I feel like my personal safety was compromised."

Alexandra laughed a little. "Don't you know who that is?" Her tone was incredulous.

"Should I?"

"That's Ke*von* Edmonds." Alexandra dropped the moniker with all the frustration one might employ when pointing out the recognition factor of, say, Bill Clinton.

But the name meant nothing to Simone. "Did he escape some grisly murder charge or something? Like O.J. Simpson?"

Alexandra shook her head. "People say he's the new Diddy. He's got a recording label, a clothing line, a reality show. The man even has his own brand of vodka."

Simone shot a glance backward. "Oh, well . . . he's still disgusting."

Alexandra sniffed. "Your package should be out soon.

Excuse me." And then she darted away to engage the ghetto mogul. "Again, I'm *so* sorry about that bag. But I know we can find something that will be just as fabulous for your friend."

Simone turned away. How vile. As she pushed thoughts of Kevon Edmonds out of mind, she attempted to do the same on the matter of her finances. After all, there were larger issues to fret over. Like what to wear on tomorrow's show. As much as she loathed to admit it, Emma Ronson had been consistently outdoing her on the fashion front. A drippy news girl! And Simone was a model and actress. Something had to give.

A beautiful Asian woman emerged with Simone's purse. It was nestled inside a rich Dior box and nestled once more inside an equally rich shopping bag. An empty place in her heart seemed to fill up when she took possession of it. Shopping for luxury items always carried that impact.

Just as Simone was slipping into a cab, her cellular vibrated. The incoming number perplexed her. "Hello?"

"Name your price, Foxy Brown. I'm the kind of brother who doesn't like to be told he can't have something."

Simone placed her hand over the mouthpiece to call out her address to the annoyed driver. "How did you get my cell number?" Her voice was humorless.

"I'm a resourceful motherfucker."

Simone stewed in a cauldron of silence, feeling violated and preyed upon. "I don't find this amusing."

"That makes two of us."

The taxi crawled along Fifty-Seventh Street. A bus showcasing the images of Simone, Sutton, Emma, and Finn on a massive promotional poster pulled up alongside in the right lane.

"Don't call me again," Simone said icily. "*Ever.*"

"That's cold, baby," Kevon cooed.

Simone could feel her heartbeat accelerate. "I'm not your baby."

"Not yet. Have dinner with me. We'll see what happens."

"When I dream about a dinner invitation, it's from George Clooney, not Snoop Dogg." With that, Simone promptly disconnected the call and speed dialed Tilly. "You won't believe what I just saw!" she launched without preamble. "My face on the side of a city bus to promote the show! It was such a weird sensation!"

"The important thing is to be pleased with the photograph," Tilly said. "I've dealt with this so many times in my career."

Simone took in a quiet breath, allowing the condescending response to evaporate. "Yes, but—"

"And if you think advertising on a bus is strange," Tilly went on, "try seeing yourself on a billboard in the middle of Times Square."

"I suppose there is no comparison," Simone shot back, somewhat acidly.

"Probably not. But I'm still thrilled for you. Finn showed me the opening show's overnight ratings at lunch this week. It's off to a very promising start. That's more than I can say for my husband's show. They just pink slipped fourteen production staffers. Any day now he's going to be unemployed."

"Well, at least he has a trust fund to fall back on," Simone said lightly. "My first paycheck disappeared instantly."

"Oh, our trust funds are earmarked for the future," Tilly remarked archly. "He still has to work. And so do I. Your problem is that you don't budget your money. You just spend, spend, spend with no regard for fiscal discipline."

Simone's grip tightened on the cellular. The nerve of this bitch! Her best friend, her enemy . . . her *frenemy*! "That would sound better coming from someone who wasn't handed the deed to a fabulous Tribeca apartment."

"That was a wedding gift," Tilly said defensively.

"A trip to Belize is a wedding gift," Simone countered. "Being given an apartment puts you on another financial planet."

"I still budget," Tilly argued.

"I can't talk to you about money."

"You can't talk to yourself about it, either. That's why you live in a constant state of denial."

The cabdriver jerked to a stop in front of Simone's building. She paid the fare and a decent tip before swinging out. "Have you ever heard of Kevon Edmonds?" She was desperate to change the subject.

"It's pronounced Ke*von*," Tilly corrected. "And yes, I have. He's a very successful entertainment mogul. But still a poor man's Jay-Z. Why?"

"He accosted me at the Christian Dior boutique, and then he had the audacity to ask me out for dinner."

"You should go," Tilly advised.

"You're not serious. He's *gross!*"

"Yes, but it would be good for your career. Especially now."

Simone dashed into a vestibule to retrieve her mail, grimacing at the thickness of two credit card statements as she boarded the elevator. "God, I would rather be seen in public with an on-duty garbage man than Kevon Edmonds."

The moment Simone stepped inside her apartment, she halted, sensing something very wrong. "Chanel?" she called out.

Nothing.

"Let me call you back," she told Tilly, hanging up as she

feverishly raced from room to room, searching for her beloved cat.

And then her cellular rang. She knew who it was. She knew what he would say, too.

"Looking for something?"

Simone's heart sank.

"I've got your pussy right here in my hand." It was Tommy Robb.

THE IT PARADE
BY JINX WIATT

Fill in the Blanks

It's no secret that ageless beauty Demi Moore went cougaring and captured hunky Ashton Kutcher in her hunter's net. She even tamed the baby-faced stud into total domestication. But at least her twenty-something lover has brains (he's outsmarted every naysayer in Hollywood) and impressive bank (his accounts are big to bursting). So it's too bad that a certain TV news diva who just hit the half-century mark and is now spewing venom on a morning chat show has to settle for a dumb-as-dirt/poor-as-dirt young buck when she moves in for the kill.

9

Sutton

Sutton walked into the Stone Rose at the Time Warner Center feeling not even a few bucks shy of a million dollars.

The Beehive was a ratings hit, Emma Ronson was itching to quit the show, and all the naysayers who swore up and down that Sutton Lancaster would recede into oblivion after leaving Fox News were eating shit on a silver platter.

She slid onto a seat at the bar and surveyed the scene, taking in the ambient lounge music, the Columbia students laughing it up at a corner table, the junior sales executives seeking refuge from their lonely hotels and sterile office environments, and the other women . . . just like her.

Some were from Connecticut, some from New Jersey, some from Manhattan—the Upper East Side, the Upper West Side. They were seasoned and well groomed and freshly Botoxed and personally trained as far as their gravity-fighting bodies could endure. And they were all here for one thing.

"What can I get you?" The hot young bartender was talking.

Sutton was listening. She smiled at him. "What would *you* order?"

"I make a Cosmo that'll make your toes curl."

"Really?"

He nodded with confidence.

"Bring it on."

"You got it."

She watched him work, instantly attracted to his lazy guy manner. Punishing sessions at the gym were not part of his agenda. He was fit but lanky, probably kept in shape by enviable metabolism and the occasional game of pick-up basketball. His hair straggled down to the nape of his neck, and the fuzz on his handsome angular face was at least three days' worth of growth.

He presented his electric pink masterpiece with a cocky grin. "One sip and you'll tell me to get started on a second round."

Sutton fingered the stem of the martini glass, seductively stroking it up and down before knocking back a greedy gulp.

The bartender waited.

Sutton savored. It was the finest Cosmo ever. "That's the best thing I've had in my mouth in a very long time."

"I've got something even better than that."

"Oh, I bet you do." She raised her drink and let out a dirty laugh.

"Another?"

"Absolutely."

"Coming right up." He went to work, pausing intermittently to flash Sutton a flirtatious smile. "I've never seen you in here before. First time?"

"First time at Stone Rose," Sutton clarified. "Not my first time at the rodeo."

He nodded up and down, impressed. "Okay, then. Good to know."

Sutton drained the last of the first Cosmo, timing it perfectly with the arrival of the second. "Cheers."

The bartender checked his watch, a cheap Timex digital. "Hey, in about five minutes I can join you."

"Who says I'm looking for company?"

He made a show out of glancing around. "Well, for starters, everyone in this bar. Should I poll the people on the sidewalk, too?" He laughed.

Sutton laughed, too. "Is it that bad?"

The bartender lifted his brow. "I don't know. Maybe it's that good. You tell me."

She stared at him for several long seconds, taking in the full impact of his easy sex appeal. "What's your name? And how long have you been able to legally drink?"

"Scooter. Three years."

Twenty-four. Sutton shook her head. "I think I'm going to need a note from your mother."

"She'll write one. After my last girlfriend? Believe me, she would do it."

"What kind of a name is *Scooter*? It makes you sound like a golden retriever."

He shrugged. "Early nickname that stuck. What's yours?"

"You don't know who I am?"

"Should I?"

"You must be one of these young people who gets their news from Jon Stewart and *The Daily Show*."

Scooter shook his head. "I work days and party at night. Hardly ever read or watch television. Sometimes I check headlines on the Net, but I prefer online porn."

"I see," Sutton remarked. "A true intellectual."

He shrugged again. "But something tells me you didn't come in here looking for a smart guy."

"No, I've had my share of those. They're definitely over-rated." The remains of Cosmo Number Two went down the hatch. A delicious buzz tingled inside Sutton's brain. She liked this bar. She liked this bartender even more.

Glancing around, she noticed other women not unlike her—well preserved and dispirited by bastards closer to their own age. She had indeed entered a den of cougars.

"Can you handle a third round?" Scooter asked.

Sutton challenged him with her eyes. "You'll quit before I will."

Scooter tilted his head, smiled, and went to work, showing off some impressive cocktail moves.

Sutton admired his beautiful hands and the impressive body they were attached to. Right away she started comparing him physically to her ex. Unfair, yes, since Scooter was almost three decades younger. But fairness never entered the equation when men operated in precisely the same fashion. Where Garrison was soft and fleshy, Scooter was hard and sinewy. There. She thought it. And it felt fantastic. The sweetest revenge.

"Keep that one cold for me," Sutton instructed. "I'll be right back." She slid off the stool and ventured toward the ladies' room, swaying slightly to the music, her cheeky mood suddenly compromised by the thought of Garrison sending Emma a flower arrangement identical to the kind he used to send her. What a lazy, unoriginal son of a bitch.

Sutton checked her face in the dimly lit mirror, finger-combing her hair a bit before applying a fresh coat of lip gloss. She looked good. *For fifty.* Goddamn the qualifiers of getting older. But who was she kidding? Garrison wanted a younger, firmer, tighter piece of ass. And Scooter probably just wanted a nice tip left on the counter. She was absolutely nowhere.

Sighing deeply, Sutton flung open the door to leave and

nearly collided with Scooter, bracing her hands on his chest to avoid impact. She could feel the heat of his skin underneath the fabric of his Oxford shirt.

"I'm betting on the fact that you can get dirty after two drinks," Scooter whispered. "How about a preview before the main event?"

Sutton took in a short, shocked breath.

"Come with me." Scooter took her by the hand and stealthily glanced around as he pulled Sutton into the men's room, clicked the lock into place, and ushered her inside a stall.

Sutton was simultaneously appalled and aroused. "I don't do it in public bathrooms. That's twenty-year-old cokehead territory."

Gently, Scooter placed his hands on her shoulders and guided her down to a sitting position on the commode. "Think of it as a chance to recapture your youth." He unhooked his leather belt with the skull-and-crossbones buckle, the weight of which dropped open his lived-in jeans.

She stared first at the elaborate ivy tattoo surrounding his belly button, then nearly gasped at the sight of his cock, only semierect yet still impressive and adorned with a large gauge circular barbell—a Prince Albert piercing. The sight was luridly fascinating. She could not take her eyes off of it.

Scooter smiled down on her. "It's not on exhibit. You can touch it. You can suck it."

"Will I get lead poisoning?" Sutton asked, only half-jokingly.

He laughed and stroked her hair. "You've never seen one of these before?"

Sutton shook her head, inspecting the jewelry's insertion points on the outside of the frenulum and then into the urethra, nearly wincing as she thought about how painful it must have been.

"It didn't hurt that much," Scooter said as if reading her mind. "It's a highly vascular part of the body, and the tissue is very elastic. The worst of it was going without sex for ten days. Now that was painful." He paused a beat. "I can take it out if you want. I'll do anything for a blow job at this point. But girls my age love it. They can't get enough."

Girls my age. In Sutton's current state of mind, those were trigger words, a challenge to prove that she was young enough, hot enough, vital enough to keep up with the baby bitches steaming up the asphalt jungle of Manhattan.

She took him in her mouth, tentatively at first, adjusting to the warring sensations of hot flesh and cold metal. And judging from Scooter's rapid breathing and soft mewls of pleasure, Sutton was catching on quite well. Maybe there was something to be said for age and experience after all.

Suddenly, there was a jangle on the bathroom door.

Sutton's heart lurched.

"It's out of order," Scooter shouted. "Come back in five."

Sutton halted her efforts.

"No, don't stop," Scooter murmured. "Everything's cool. Everything's fine. Keep going. I'm almost there."

Sutton continued on, out of desire more than anything else. The urgent, unsavory quality of the encounter pushed her to perform at the peak of her abilities. She wanted this young buck to remember her as one of the best. Hopefully, he would brag about it to his buddies. And then the next time they passed by a woman like her on a crowded sidewalk, maybe they would think twice before looking through her as if she were past her prime and not even there.

This one was for the girls.

THE IT PARADE
BY *JINX WIATT*

Fill in the Blanks

Some girls have all the luck. That delicious news anchor turned morning talk show host deserves a far better specimen of man on her Pilates-sculpted arm. First, her whirlwind romance with America's prince ended with him going for a quickie marriage (his second) and baby (his first—that we know of!). Now her latest romance (with a much older media magnate) could be on the rocks if she ever finds out what goes on in the back of his limousine during the A.M. drive from penthouse to office.

10

Emma

"You have *got* to get over this . . . get over *him*," Delilah said, tipping back her third glass of wine.

"Don't you think I know that?" Emma cried. "I'm not wallowing out of self-pity or self-indulgence. I just can't shake him off. God, what is wrong with me?"

Delilah gave her a quizzical look. "I have no idea." One beat. "Was the sex that good?"

"Yes . . . I mean, no . . . I mean, yes, the sex was good, but that's not the only reason. It was him. I've never responded to a man like that before. He reached me on almost every level. And he's such a jerk. So, ultimately, what does that say about me?"

"That you're a very self-aware . . . twit," Delilah offered cheerily.

Emma rolled her eyes. "Oh, that's nice. Says the woman who hasn't made it past a third date with the same guy in . . . how many years?"

"Two. And that's only because I don't suffer fools."

"Right, right," Emma murmured, swirling her wine. "You have absolutely no issues of your own to speak of."

"I'm not the one sniveling like some bitter old cow. *You're* the one in crisis. We're analyzing you tonight."

"Well, fine, but at least *try* to be a bit supportive."

Delilah picked up a sequined throw pillow and tossed it in Emma's direction. "I can't *do* supportive. You know that. What am I supposed to say? 'Oh, there, there, one day your prince will come back to you.'"

"Once in a while, something like that would be nice," Emma countered.

Delilah shook her head. "I can't do the enabling thing. Even on a total bullshit level. It's just not in me." She dipped a Thai spring roll into a spicy mango sauce and wolfed it down.

It was Saturday night, a standing date for them to indulge in Netflix, takeout food, and catching up. So here they were, ensconced inside Delilah's Greenwich Village studio, already half-drunk and arguing like teenage sisters who share the same closet.

"Maybe we should go out," Emma suggested.

"On a Saturday night?" Delilah fired back. "Are you insane? I cede this night to the bridge-and-tunnel crowd. Besides, in your current state the risk is there for you to fall for New Jersey's version of Dean Paul."

"Hmmm," Emma murmured with faux interest. "I'm intrigued. What is New Jersey's version?"

"I'm sure that he wears cologne, earrings, and hair gel. I'm sure that his parents own a small chain of Subway shops or something. And I'm sure that you would think the barbed wire tattoo around his arm was really hot." Pleased with herself, Delilah drank up and poured herself more wine, topping off Emma as well. "Am I right?"

"Probably," Emma grumbled.

"This thing with the Jewish grandfather is obviously doing

nothing for you. I say end it. Spend some time alone. Go on a man diet. Trust me. It'll clear your head."

Emma regarded Delilah for a moment.

"By the way, that's me being all treacly."

"I know. And it's so . . . revealing of your emotional incapability."

"I had a cat once," Delilah argued, laughing at herself. "But she threw up a hairball on my brand-new flokati rug, so I gave her away."

Emma grinned. "You're right, though. I'm not being fair to Garrison."

"Screw Garrison!" Delilah thundered. "Think about yourself. That's the important thing. You're not being fair to you."

Emma fell silent.

"It must make it hurt more, you know? To be with someone you don't really want to be with just to avoid being alone. That's worse than actually being alone."

"Maybe you're right," Emma whispered.

"Do you want the rest of that?" Delilah asked as she reached for the last carton of Thai fried rice.

"Go ahead. I'm done."

Delilah proceeded to work the chopsticks like a pro. "But it must be hard trying to get over an ex-boyfriend when he's constantly showing up in the *New York Post* with his wife and new baby. That's got to suck."

Emma drank deep on her wine. "Do I hear an actual note of sympathy coming from Delilah Krause?"

"Am I going soft? Whatever you do, don't tell the writing staff at *Laugh Track*." She paused a beat. "Or go right ahead. They'll never believe you."

Emma smiled.

"But let's talk about something. Here you are mooning

over Dean Paul Lockhart, and he could—shock of all shocks—be gay."

Emma shook her head. "Delilah, please."

"I'm just reading between the lines from what's been in the columns. And where there's smoke . . ."

"So he's friends with Finn. Big deal. Lots of straight guys have gay friends."

"But why?"

"Delilah, get out of that sophomoric writers' room for a minute. It's not that unusual."

"Unless he's working out a latent curiosity."

"You're impossible."

"All I'm saying is that could be another sound reason to move on. Think about it. He's a cad. He's no stranger to getting married, even though I'd still classify him as a commitment-phobe. And now he might be bisexual. Emma, this guy is *Manthrax*. Run for your life!"

"You can't believe what's in the columns. Most of it is total crap."

"Do you dismiss those hints about his marriage to Tilly being on the rocks?" Delilah asked. "Or do those accounts actually give you some hope?"

"I really hate you right now."

Delilah shrugged. "You said you wanted to talk. We're talking. If you want to bullshit, I'm not the girl for that."

Emma steadied her wineglass on the coffee table and sank back on the sofa, burying her face in her hands. "God, I'm such a mess."

"Well, if the dream is to one day marry Dean Paul, then you need a new dream. *Immediately*. It would make you the stepmother to a child named Cantaloupe. What more reason do you need to move on?"

Emma laughed a little. "You're awful."

"I'm also right. You have to steel yourself. If the marriage trouble talk is true, then watch out. *Hollywood Live* is failing, too. Don't think you can save him, either. Because you'll get caught up all over again. And you'll get hurt all over again, too. He'll just use you to get through the rough patch, and you'll be back to square one."

"You sound so sure," Emma murmured.

"I am. My relationship résumé might be spotty, but I understand men. I know how they think. I spend countless hours with them in the writers' room for brainstorming sessions that last days. Literally. We pull all-nighters all the time. It's like reading an X-ray of the male psyche. In fact, if I were a smarter woman, I'd be a lesbian right now."

Emma laughed again, this time from the gut.

"Oh, you think I'm kidding. But I'm totally serious."

"No, I believe you."

Delilah finished off the Thai fried rice, and opened up yet another bottle of wine—the third of the night. She sloshed both of their glasses up to the rim and giggled. "This is fun."

"For you maybe."

"For both of us. Don't worry. If we don't have you sorted out by the time we finish this bottle, then . . . well, then we'll just have to open up another one."

"Let's go out," Emma said. "I can't sit here and drink all night. I'll pass out on the couch."

"So? You've crashed here before."

"I know, but I'm already fading. I need some air and new scenery. There has to be some club in town that's not over-run with commuter riffraff."

Delilah considered the situation. "We could try Retox. The door is murder. Sometimes too tough for me alone, but the two of us should have no trouble getting in." She shrugged. "I'm game if you are."

Emma thought about it. "Let's go. If we stay here and watch
Legends of the Fall for the gazillionth time I'll be asleep before
the opening credits."

Delilah stood up. "Okay, party girl. It's on." She disappeared into the bedroom for a moment, emerging to toss out
a vintage Sex Pistols T-shirt. "Lose the cashmere. This is a rock
club."

Emma stripped off the sweater and replaced it with the
long-sleeved tee. Now with her boots and drainpipe-fitted
jeans, all she had to do was add hot water and stir for instant
punk rock priestess.

Delilah stepped over to inspect. "You're almost there, daytime girl. But the soft pink mouth gives you away." Ceremon-
iously, she presented a dark tube of lipstick.

Emma glanced down, noticed the color was called
Grunge Whore, but swiped some on anyway. "Do I pass?"

Delilah nodded. "Like a Motley Crue groupie."

Emma grinned. "You would know." And Delilah Krause
did. Though her exploits did not quite make it into the pages
of *The Dirt*, the band's notorious rock autobiography of sex,
drugs, and extreme excess, among her premium achievements
were the bragging rights of bedding down both Vince Neil
and Nikki Sixx—on separate occasions, of course.

They tumbled into a cab and swung out on West Twenty-
Eighth Street in Chelsea. A long line of club hopefuls clogged
the sidewalk.

Emma groaned, her sudden burst of night energy morph-
ing into fatigue. "It's a clusterfuck."

"Come with me," Delilah commanded, taking Emma's
hand and stalking past those waiting in queue and moving directly toward a doorman who wore a very discerning expression on his face.

"We just improved your hot girl ratio," Delilah announced.

"Plus, we've got cool jobs. I write for *Laugh Track*, and she hosts a new morning talk show."

The doorman gave her a smug look.

"I know. I'm wondering the same thing. Is this club good enough for us?"

This last bit made him break a smile, and suddenly, they were being waved inside the intimate rock haunt with its deep red lighting, snakeskin furniture, and black crystal chandeliers.

The D.J. slammed the crowd full throttle with "Rock the Casbah" by The Clash.

"What are we drinking?" Emma shouted.

"I've got it covered!" Delilah hollered back. Within moments, she was pushing into Emma's hand a strange brew of vanilla vodka, pineapple juice, sour mix, lime juice, and milk that the club had christened the Horny Goat.

Emma recoiled at first, then chased down the tasty concoction as easily as vitamin water. "This was a great idea!" she squealed, gyrating her hips to the turgid rock beat. "I needed this!"

Her gaze swept up and around, across the black-and-white West Coast rock scene images lining the walls, then onto the packed dance floor of rock disciples. She noticed a young peroxide beauty channeling Debbie Harry from her hottest Blondie era. She also noticed the man grinding against her.

It was Dean Paul Lockhart.

She glanced back to see Delilah swaying obliviously to the music, both hands sweeping in the air, feeling no pain.

But Emma Ronson was suddenly hurting bad.

THE IT PARADE
BY JINX WIATT

Fill in the Blanks

You know the old saying. *Ex* marks the spot. And sometimes it's a nasty one. Morning television's hottest new gay star (the coffee and muffin time slot is *the* place to be for those in entertainment who live life out and proud) is reeling from the are-they-or-aren't-they rumors about his very married BFF. Now who should turn back up but his scandal-plagued former boyfriend, a super creep who presented himself as Steven Spielberg's nephew and mooched off every worthwhile restaurant and bar in Manhattan. Will bygones be bygones?

11
Finn

It amazed him. How much time he could daydream away analyzing the situation with Dean Paul. The situation that did exist. The situation that might exist. The situation that he hoped could exist. These thoughts often occupied Finn for hours.

He checked his mobile again. Yes, the signal remained strong and clear. The problem was that you could not psychically *will* someone to return your call. Or rather your last five unanswered calls. But who was counting?

Finn just lay there in the dark, wondering what the hell to do with himself, knowing that something had to give. It was ridiculous to carry on like this, to be a prisoner of this secret paralysis. But only one thing could cure it. A phone call, an e-mail, or a text. Any simple sign that Finn had not been banished from Dean Paul's life could always snap him back to the land of the living.

The vibration of his mobile caused Finn's heart to lurch. He clamored to check the ID screen, spirits crashing upon realization that the incoming call was coming from Tilly's cellular. Disappointed but still curious, he picked up. "Hi, Tilly."

"Finn!" Tilly exclaimed. "Thank God you picked up. I had this fear that you would be at some gay disco and not hear your phone."

"No such luck," Finn remarked.

Tilly bulldozed on. "Have you heard from Dean Paul? He's not picking up his cell, and I have no idea where he is."

"Same here," Finn answered, feeling a moment of pure solidarity. "I've called him a couple of times and haven't heard back."

"Well, this is so irresponsible," Tilly hissed. "Don't you think? I mean, what if there was an emergency with Cantaloupe?"

"Is everything okay with the baby?" Finn asked.

"Yes, of course," Tilly assured him. "I'm just speaking hypothetically. Horror of all horrors, what if something *did* happen? I shouldn't have to go on a scavenger hunt for my husband and the father of my child on a Saturday night. He ought to pick up on the first ring. As far as I'm concerned, this is tantamount to spousal and child abuse!"

Finn rolled his eyes. Only Tilly could make such a dramatic leap. "Well, if I hear from him tonight, I'll tell him to call you."

"Don't bother," Tilly huffed. "If he doesn't call me soon, then I'm turning off all the phones anyway."

"So how is Cantaloupe?"

"Oh, she's an angel as always," Tilly answered in a singsong voice. "I missed her bunches today. Veronika took her out to a mommy-and-me class and then to a checkup with the pediatrician. Now she's reading her a bedtime story. I've scarcely had a moment with my own child the whole day!"

Finn was speechless. Why would Tilly assign the nanny to all of these intimate maternal duties? But he did not give voice to the question.

"You're so great with children, Finn," Tilly went on. "They adore you so. Have you ever thought about adopting a puppy?"

"A *puppy*?"

"Well, yes," Tilly replied. "I think that's a nice compromise. I just don't believe that gays should adopt or have children through high-tech fertility means. I'm a firm believer in the traditional nuclear family—mother, father—"

"And *nanny*," Finn cut in acidly.

"Oh, God, yes," Tilly said, not picking up on the hostility. "It's impossible to raise a child without one."

"But people do it all the time," Finn said. "Maybe they think of their children as actual people, though, and not fashion accessories."

"I'm so glad to hear you talk about family values," Tilly gushed. "Most gay men are such decadent pleasure seekers." She sighed. "I have to run, Finn. My La Prairie cleansing mask has stayed on far too long and it's hardening into cement. Please call if that awful husband of mine happens to reveal his whereabouts. Bye-bye." *Click.*

Finn stared at his mobile in absolute disbelief. Could he really blame Dean Paul for being unfaithful to that woman? His stomach knotted up in anxiety at the thought. Is that where Dean Paul was tonight? Having an affair?

A sudden storm of jealousy raged inside Finn's heart. Why did he feel like Dean Paul was cheating on him, too? What a strange response. This situation was beyond fucked up.

Sometimes Finn hated himself for the complicated feelings that Dean Paul stirred within. And other times he gave himself a break and just tried to manage them as best as he could.

He worked like hell to treat the relationship as nothing more than a platonic friendship, but feelings always crept in to complicate. His reactions to simple gestures and behaviors ran him up and down the emotional scale.

Dean Paul wielded an uncanny and unprecedented power over him. A casual phone call carrying an invitation to exercise or grab lunch could send Finn's spirits soaring through the sky. And a failure to return calls—such as the ones Finn had made over the last few days—could send him down into the depths.

What they shared was an easy friendship. Finn had become a B-list substitute for the straight guy buddies that Tilly had forced Dean Paul to give up. Intellectually, Finn knew the score. But emotionally, he could not stop himself from reacting to every moment as if it were a love affair. Maybe because in some pathetic way, that is precisely what it was. At least for Finn.

He sensed that Dean Paul was well aware of his effect on him, too. Someone that narcissistic could not exist in the dark about that. Plus, it explained Dean Paul's penchant for occasionally acknowledging the unspoken feelings and raising the bar in an off-color, humorous way that simultaneously titillated Finn and twisted a knife in his heart.

It'd serve her right if you were sucking my cock whenever we got together.

Who knows? Next time I cheat, maybe it'll be with you.

At the end of the day, it was all a joke to Dean Paul. Still, Finn surmised that there was some kind of reciprocal attraction. He had danced around flirtations with enough men to know. It was an attraction that would never be acted upon. Not in a million years. But it was there. And just knowing that triggered in Finn a craving for proximity on any terms.

Sometimes Dean Paul would get bold and say the most

outrageous things just to see what kind of reaction he could provoke in Finn. At other times he seemed uncomfortable, maybe even ashamed, and he disappeared for days at a time, ignoring all contact. The inconsistency was torture. But Finn came back for more again and again. Dean Paul had become like a drug. And Finn was an addict refusing to go to rehab.

He wondered if Jinx Wiatt's snarky column mentions had played a part in Dean Paul's latest attempt at going AWOL. That bitch's blind item gossip teases were written in twenty/twenty vision. It was the easiest guessing game in town.

Finn's mobile vibrated again. He felt another surge of hope in his heart as he reached for it. The incoming number was unidentified and rang no bells. "Hello?"

"It's been a long time, babe. Do you know who this is?" The thrashing sounds of Hole's "Celebrity Skin" blasted in the background.

Finn shut his eyes. "Benjamin Fitzpatrick."

"Bingo! You must miss me." He laughed. "Actually, I go by Benji now. Benji Patt. It's shorter and looks better in bold-face in the columns."

"Really? I haven't noticed a single mention."

"Keep reading," Benji shouted over the music.

The cocky edge to his voice instantly annoyed Finn. Shit. He sure could pick the right guys to fall in love with. Benjamin the flim-flam fag and Dean Paul the heartbreaker. What a track record.

"Congratulations on the talk show," Benji went on. "That's awesome. I've only caught it once. But you're a natural."

"Thanks," Finn replied flatly.

"I've got some projects in the works. They just haven't been announced yet."

"By *announced yet*, does that mean by you or by law enforcement?"

"*Meow*," Benji mocked in reply. "Retract your claws."

Finn just lay there, steaming in the silence.

Benjamin Fitzpatrick was his most significant ex-boyfriend, a relationship that lasted almost a year, until it was revealed that the guy was a fraud and a con artist, passing himself off as Steven Spielberg's nephew and bilking bars, restaurants, and boutiques out of free drinks, dinners, and merchandise all over Manhattan. Finn had felt such guilt and embarrassment by association that he spent thousands of dollars to make restitution.

"I did the Miami thing for a while," Benji trilled. "Then spent some time in Austin and L.A. But I missed New York. So I'm back."

"Great. Who are you pretending to be this time? Paris Hilton's half brother?"

"I'm through with those games," Benji insisted. "I don't need to be someone else. I can make things happen on my own now."

Finn merely shook his head. Benji was smoking hot and a consummate charmer and manipulator. But he was also full of shit. At least there was an upside to this surprise phone call. Finn was experiencing no residual feelings whatsoever. In fact, his central nervous system response to the entire exchange was a total flatline.

"What's up with you?" Benji asked. "Are the rumors true? Have you become a homewrecker?"

"Take care, Benji," Finn said dismissively. "I'll look for your name in boldface." He started to hang up.

"Because I'm here at Retox watching your boyfriend right now, and it looks like he's getting ready to seriously wreck some blonde rocker chick."

Finn stayed on the line, his heart pounding all of a sudden.

"I've got the whole thing on cell phone video," Benji said proudly. "I figure TMZ will make me a sweet offer."

"I'll make you a better one."

"Then you better hurry your ass over here."

THE IT PARADE
BY JINX WIATT

Fill in the Blanks

They say opposites attract. The cowboy and the lady. The blue collar hunk and the pampered city girl. And so on. But who on earth could have imagined that oh-so-snotty Black American Princess linking arms and tipping back Cristal with hip-hop's reigning kingpin mogul? One thing is certain. She better trade her Pilates classes for kickboxing. Why? Those around-the-way girls who are never shy about moving in on another woman's man definitely know how to fight.

12
Simone

"I'm not coming up!" Simone screamed. "Bring Chanel downstairs to the lobby right now, or I'm calling the police! *Seriously*, Tommy, I will call them!"

"Excuse me, I'm going to have to ask you to keep your voice down," the uniformed doorman scolded her.

Fighting back tears of frustration and rage, Simone ignored him. "I hate you, Tommy! I fucking hate you!"

Discreetly, the doorman gestured to a security guard. Within seconds, he stepped over to Simone and took firm possession of her arm. "Miss, please exit the building immediately."

Simone shook free of his hold. "Get your hands off me! That crazy son of a bitch has my cat! He's got my cat!"

But the shocked faces staring back at her—belonging to the doorman, the security guard, and a few residents passing through the lobby—seemed to indicate that the only crazy person in the building was Simone.

The doorman swiped the front desk telephone receiver from her hand and engaged in a brief, hushed conversation with Tommy before hanging up as the rent-a-cop half-pulled, half-escorted Simone toward the exit door.

All of a sudden, she was standing on the sidewalk, bawling as if the world had ended.

Passersby walked onward with little interest.

Simone just stood there, crying convulsively and wracking her brain about what to do next. Tommy's theft of Chanel had occurred a few days ago. Since then, he had put her off with phone tag games and scheduled meetings that never materialized.

Raw with nerves, she glanced upward to Tommy's penthouse level apartment. "Chanel!" she called out desperately, tears streaming down her face.

It was the violation and sense of powerlessness that had Simone so upset. The thought of Tommy hurting Chanel never entered her mind. Even now she was dangerously close to the edge. Going there would certainly tip her over. And so she refused to consider it. Simone was giving Tommy Robb just enough credit. Psycho bastards like him must have limits. Stopping short of cruelty to animals had to be one of them.

Feeling more vulnerable than ever and not knowing where to turn, she called Tilly, operating under the extravagant hope that the woman could offer some advice or even a moment of comfort.

"Simone, please make it quick," Tilly snapped right away. "The timing of this call couldn't be worse."

"I still don't have Chanel," Simone cried. "Tommy won't give her back. I don't—"

"You have a missing cat," Tilly cut in. "Okay, *I* have a missing husband and father. Dean Paul is nowhere to be found. The columns seem to suggest that I could find him in Finn's bed. But apparently that's not the case. I've already checked with him."

"How long has he been gone?" Simone asked.

"I haven't seen him since early this morning."

Simone felt the urge to throw her cellular into the gutter. What a self-absorbed bitch! This was hardly a future plotline for *Without a Trace*. But she played along. "Are you worried?"

"No, I'm pissed off," Tilly shot back. "And anger is bad for future lines around the mouth, so I'm slathering on the La Mer cream as we speak." One beat. "You sound terrible. Are you crying?"

"Security just kicked me out of Tommy's building," Simone said tearfully.

"Simone, please!" Tilly exclaimed. "You said he was stalking you. Now it sounds like you're stalking him."

"Tilly, he kidnapped my cat!"

"Honestly, Simone, this is not a grown-up situation. I'm an adult woman with a child to raise and a husband who's about to be unemployed. I have real problems to deal with." *Click.*

For a moment, Simone just stood there, fuming on the sidewalk. And then she let out a primal scream with the words, "Why am I friends with that bitch?"

Simone's cellular buzzed. If it was Tilly calling back, then she was *not* going to pick up. No such worry. But the incoming number stumped her. "Hello?"

"This is your last chance, baby girl. I never have to ask twice, but for you I'm making an exception," Kevon Edmonds said.

"I can't talk right now," Simone managed to say, mildly annoyed by the call but not revolted like she had been the other day.

"You sound stressed out," Kevon said, his voice down an octave and the closest thing to real concern she had heard since the ordeal happened. "What's wrong?"

Simone opened her mouth to offer some vague answer, then suddenly burst into tears.

"Everything's cool, baby. I got your back. Everything's cool," Kevon said in a buttery voice that provided instant comfort. "I'm rolling, and I'm coming straight to you. Tell me where you are."

Simone hesitated.

"I'm rolling straight to you, baby. Tell me where you are."

Finally, she relented and called out Tommy's Park Avenue address.

"Just chill right there. Do you hear me? Chill right there."

"Okay," Simone agreed meekly. Doing so flooded her with a sense of relief. Someone was taking charge. Someone besides her. It was a strange yet glorious feeling.

Simone waited for almost fifteen minutes. And then a 2008 H2 Hummer limousine coasted into view like a luxury liner. The front license plate emblazoned with the letters KEVONE dazzled obscenely with flashing white lights and sparkling rhinestones.

A rear door lurched open.

Simone peeked inside to see Kevon, cell phone planted to ear, nestled alone in a cabin built for at least sixteen passengers.

Silently, Kevon waved her into his sanctuary. "Listen, this big nose nigga can smell, and I'm not signing off on this shit until it's right and tight. You know what I'm saying? Nobody's going to buy perfume that smells like nasty ass pussy. I said I wanted that shit to smell like honeysuckle and cotton candy, and that punk ass bitch from Lancaster shows up with a bottle of nasty pussy spray. What the fuck is that? Work this out for me. Next time they call a meeting to sample a product with my name on it, I want to know that it's in the hands of people who care about my rep. Now I got a situation here that needs my attention. Peace out."

He reached over to shut the door behind her, cocooning them inside his purple pleasure palace on wheels.

Simone sank deep into the silver leather banquette.

"Tell me all about it, baby girl," Kevon said. "You got problems. I got solutions. Trust that."

Simone believed him, and the relief of hearing those words nearly overwhelmed her. Far from being all cried out, tears sprang to her eyes again. The desperate yearning to be cared for conjured up old childhood demons.

She had been an international model at fifteen, a young woman on her own in Paris. And then on her own again when her parents' lives imploded, and they embezzled every dollar she had ever earned to stave off their own financial ruin. It was always Simone looking out for Simone. Rarely had she ever had someone strong and capable to turn to.

Even during the best of times with Tommy Robb, he was hardly a source of support. The bastard was selfish and possessive and cheap as shit. His money belonged only to him and his pig of a mother. Any woman who expected more than an occasional dinner out was a gold-digging whore. So Simone was open to chivalry any way a man chose to offer it. And at this particular moment, that included ghetto style.

"Tommy Robb took my cat, Chanel," Simone announced.

Kevon gave her an assuring smile. "Don't worry, baby girl. We'll get your kitty back." His tone was absolute.

Simone just stared at him.

"Why'd he do something like that?"

"Because he's a crazy son of a bitch."

Kevon grinned. "Now I believe you could make a son of a bitch go crazy. With your fine ass. I definitely believe that."

"Don't make me regret getting in this limo," Simone said quietly, noticing a bottle of Cristal iced down in a silver bucket.

He picked up on her distraction. "You want some bubbly?" He proceeded to do the honors before she could answer.

The cork popped as loud as a gunshot.

Kevon filled a crystal flute up to the top and presented it to her like the gift that it was.

Simone drank the champagne all the way down, then held out her empty glass for more. "I broke things off last year. On New Year's Eve, as a matter of fact. And it's been hell ever since. Not in terms of regrets. That was the best way to start the year—without him. But he won't leave me alone. He kept coming into my apartment until I had the locks changed. I've changed my cell number half a dozen times." She shook her head. "He always manages to find out what it is. He's a spokesman for AT&T. Maybe that's how he does it. I guess I should be with T-Mobile or something." She laughed a little and tipped back her flute. "I used to live on this stuff. Back when I was a model. Cristal and cigarettes. I could run on that for days."

She felt herself relax. The alcohol was going straight to her head for a tingling buzz, and the emotional turmoil seemed to be subsiding. Kevon had said he would get her kitty back. Somehow she knew that to be true.

"Tommy's not relentless," Simone continued. "But he's persistent. I hear he's that way with any girl who breaks up with *him*. I guess his ego can't handle it. His harassment comes and goes, and just when you think it's over for good, he comes back with more. But this business with Chanel is way over the line. I've been a wreck."

"How did he get hold of your cat if you changed the locks?" Kevon asked.

Simone rolled her eyes. "He's Tommy Robb. He plays outfield for the New York Yankees. There was a new super in my building who didn't know our messy history. All it took was a good story and a signed baseball."

"Shit, I'm Kevon Edmonds, baby. It takes less than that for me to open sesame. This is where Robb lives, right?"

Simone nodded.

"Is that motherfucker home right now?"

She nodded again.

"I say we wait right here and keep getting our Cristal on until he goes out tonight. Then I'll slip inside that crib and get your cat back."

Simone's eyes widened. "You don't understand. I can't go in there. Security tossed me out not even thirty minutes ago."

"Relax, baby girl. You don't have to. Chill here. I'll work it."

"This is insane."

Kevon topped her champagne. "It's all good." He paused a beat. "If I get your kitty back, though, you have to let me take you out to dinner. Deal?"

She found herself smiling at Kevon and clinking glasses with him. "Deal."

For the next hour Simone drank, waited, and watched for Tommy while Kevon tried to impress her with newly mastered tracks from his upcoming CD, *The Black Man Cometh*. She tried to give the music a chance, but it sounded like so much of the ubiquitous hip-hop dreck already out there.

Kevon bobbed his head to his own beat. "You dig it?"

Simone could feel the half smile freeze on her face. Over a lilting groove (sampled from the Teddy Pendergrass classic "Turn Off the Lights"), Kevon was attempting to sexy rap a song called "Couples Massage" while a woman wailed orgasmic moans in the background. Hmm. Did she dig it?

"It's interesting," Simone managed to say politely. "But I'm more of a Michael Bublé and Peter Cincotti type of girl."

Kevon gave her a blank stare.

"They're two young artists with sort of a retro-Sinatra vibe," Simone explained.

Now Kevon was nodding knowingly. "Sinatra? That motherfucker's the shit."

Simone grinned at him. On some level, his street vernacular had a certain charm. He spoke from the depths of his hip-hop heart. She had to respect that. Kevon was intriguing, too. He sounded like the thug next door, but his success was undeniable.

That a perfume with his name on it was in development at Lancaster spoke volumes about his popularity and ability to parlay his personal brand far beyond the music scene milieu. The company was a prestige label for Coty and responsible for fragrances by Calvin Klein, Jennifer Lopez, Vera Wang, and Sarah Jessica Parker.

Suddenly, the enormity of Kevon's achievements began to marvel her. Simone had no delusions about her own career. For years she had carved out semi-success on the fringe with B-level modeling assignments, the occasional commercial, and small speaking roles on crime dramas. Now she had a major part in a bigger thing with *The Beehive*, but most of the critics had labeled her the weakest and most disposable of the four hosts. Yet Kevon Edmonds managed to climb his way to the top in virtually every arena.

"How did you get here?" Simone asked. Her tone was close to being awe-struck.

"How did I get *here*?" Kevon teased. "I told my man up there to drive. That's how."

Simone smiled. "You know what I mean."

Kevon drank deep, kicked back, spread his legs, and adjusted himself. "Growing up, I used to go to the library and read about these Hollywood cats. You know, the old school motherfuckers who started in the mail room and ended up running the studio. I wanted to be that cat. Nobody's going to let niggas run Hollywood, but we can damn sure run the record business. So I took a page from those West Coast cats. I did street marketing for Death Row when I was still in high school. Stupid shit like tacking up fliers and posters for Snoop Dogg's first album. My philosophy was that I could learn a little something-something from every motherfucker I met. The executives taught me shit. The buttoned-up punk from accounting taught me shit. The receptionists taught me shit. Everybody. I soaked it all up for years until I could run my own motherfucking company. And here I am. Chilling on top."

Simone felt her eyelids grow heavy. She had guzzled champagne on an empty stomach, and the impact was manifesting itself in a foggy, delicious fatigue. This idle limousine was so comfortable . . . so quiet and safe. She just wanted to stretch out for a moment and listen to Kevon tell her more about his life. Oh, yes, that would be lovely. Why was she here exactly?

"Check it," Kevon said, pointing to the sidewalk.

Simone glanced up to see Tommy Robb strutting away from the building, flanked by two bar trash sluts with stripper bodies and corner prostitute fashion sense.

Kevon gestured to his driver, a hulkish man with a bull neck. "I can have my boy fuck him up a little bit. Just say the word."

Simone half-considered the offer. In all honesty, it was tempting. *Very* tempting. "Just get my cat back for me."

"You got it, baby girl." Kevon swung out and pimp walked his way into the megabucks high-rise as if he owned the whole block.

And that was the last thing Simone remembered before waking up the next morning at the Mercer Hotel. She was still in last night's clothes, and her head throbbed with the punishment of Cristal's revenge. But sleeping down by her feet and purring like a small motor was her feline friend, safe and sound. Lovingly, Simone reached out to stroke her.

In response, Chanel stretched out lazily, purring louder.

Atop the pillow next to Simone was a small black Chanel box dressed up in white ribbon. Groggily, she opened the gift. It was a collar. Crushed black velvet with a Chanel logo glistening in crystals. Perfectly sized for her beloved pet. She smiled.

Apparently, gangstas were the new gentlemen. Who knew?

THE IT PARADE
BY JINX WIATT

Fill in the Blanks

Lady chic or biker chick? A certain news diva obviously reeling from a recent birthday that sent her careening past the half-century mark is bypassing the classy St. John duds in favor of things from Leather Tuscadero's closet. Somebody must tell Miss Not-So-Young that the skull-and-crossbones look only serves as a reminder that she is indeed closer to the grave than the tight-bodied trendy tramps she's emulating. Oops, better be careful. Why? I just got booked on this tragic case's talk show to plug my new self-help manifesto, *Ex Marks The Spot: How to Know When You're Really Over Him.* If every woman who *needed* this book—and I just mean the ones in Manhattan—actually bought a copy, I could retire for life!

13
Sutton

"Do you have any Pop-Tarts? Man, I'd love a fucking Pop-Tart right now. Either strawberry or grape. With the frosting and sprinkles on it. That'd be awesome."

Sutton was just opening her eyes.

"This one's pretty cool," Scooter said, zapping up the volume on the flat screen with the remote control. "Peter makes a volcano that shoots mud all over Marcia's new friends." He laughed.

Sutton experienced a burning sense of exposure. She had never even allowed Garrison to see her first thing in the morning. And he was considerably older.

Scooter glanced over with a sexy smile. "Do you want coffee or cock, sleepyhead? I don't want to make assumptions. Some people are set in a morning routine." He turned his attention back to TV Land and *The Brady Bunch.*

Sutton just lay there, mortified, wondering when this *boy* would realize that he had woken up with a wretched old hag on a Sunday morning.

"Man, this mattress is amazing. I could stay in bed all day. I sleep on a futon and usually wake up with a crick in my neck. How much does one of these cost?"

"Forty-five."

"Forty-five hundred for a mattress?"

"Forty-five thousand."

"Whoa. Too rich for me. Guess I'll just have to keep fucking you."

"It's by Hastens. They're hand-crafted in Sweden." Self-consciously, Sutton slid out of bed and carried the twisted top sheet with her, mummifying her body to cover almost every inch of flesh as she made her way to the privacy of the bathroom.

It took a moment of courage to face the mirror. When she did, the face that stared back was smudged with makeup but uncharacteristically vibrant and glowing. If this is what the best sex of your life could do for a fifty-year-old woman, then she wanted more of it. Lots more.

She splashed with cold water to remove the makeup streaks and rinsed with a strong mouthwash to freshen her breath. Last night Scooter had put her through quite a sexual workout. His staying power was relentless, and his creativity in the area of positions was intoxicating. In fact, the classic missionary method never even occurred to him. Sutton wondered if it was simply too traditional for such an inventive lover.

Feeling emboldened, she stepped back into the bedroom, still draped with the top sheet but now putting forth far less effort to cover every inch of skin.

Scooter remained captivated by *The Brady Bunch*. He had a thin blanket thrown casually across his waist. No matter, the imprint of his impressive cock and Prince Albert piercing was still visible.

Sutton smiled at him. "We don't have to watch children's shows. *Meet the Press* is on."

"Is that some kind of game show?" Scooter asked.

"You've never heard of *Meet the Press*?" She tried to control the incredulity in her tone. She failed.

Unashamed, Scooter shook his head. "My test for everything is whether or not they've made a Xbox game out of it. If the answer's no, it's probably lame shit."

Sutton took a few provocative steps toward him. Oh, to be young, dumb, and working in the service industry. How gloriously simple life must be. "Okay . . . back to your question from earlier."

He grinned. "About whether you want cock or coffee?"

Sutton nodded. "You should know that I don't drink caffeine on the weekends." Then she dropped the sheet to the floor, fully exposing herself. And damn proud to do it.

"I'm still craving a Pop-Tart," Scooter said almost an hour later.

Sutton was deliriously satisfied, exhausted, and ready to go back to sleep. "I don't have any Pop-Tarts," she managed in a breathless, dreamy voice. "I might have some bran-fortified cereal."

Scooter laughed, slapping her bare bottom with the palm of his hand.

Sutton squealed in response.

"I could get used to this."

She rolled onto her back and immediately cursed herself for procrastinating about the breast lift procedure. In a sudden show of modesty, she covered herself. "Used to what?"

"This mattress . . . this big apartment . . . cable TV . . . fucking you whenever I want." One beat. "But not necessarily in that order." He threaded his hand through hers, brought it to his lips, and began to suck on her fingers.

Sutton moaned softly in response. "What do you want? Drawer space and your own key?"

Scooter halted. "Maybe. Is that so wrong?"

Sutton reclaimed her hand abruptly.

"I'm kidding," Scooter assured her. "Don't get uptight on me. Up until now, you've been full of hell."

She tried to relax.

"Besides, it's no big deal. I can go back to that roach-infested closet I share with a meth addict."

"We all have our battles," Sutton whispered.

Scooter chortled and stretched out, cradling the back of his head with his hands. Not one for modesty, he just lay there—naked, tattooed, and pierced.

She reached out to finger the silver barbell adorning the equipment that had brought her such exquisite pleasure. "How much did that hurt?"

"Not as much as you'd think. Do you want your clit done? Because I know a guy."

The mere thought caused Sutton to physically recoil.

Scooter laughed. "I was drunk when I did. My girlfriend was supposed to get her clit pierced at the same time. I went first. She tossed her cookies *and* chickened out. The whole thing was her idea, too. We broke up before it even healed."

Sutton could not stop staring. "It's fascinating."

Scooter grinned, obviously pleased with himself. "You're fascinated with my cock? That's not such a bad thing." He laughed again. "Whenever I hook up with a girl, we usually spend a lot of time talking about my dick. If every man knew that, they'd all be walking around with a Prince Albert." He winked at her. "So how did you get so rich?"

"I'm not rich," Sutton protested lightly. "Not at all. At least not by any New York standard."

Scooter zeroed in on her with a give-me-a-break look. "You sleep on a mattress that costs forty-five grand."

"I've done well for myself. I can indulge now and then. But I'm not rich."

"Well, shit, what's middle class to you—the homeless?"

"Let's not talk about money."

"Why? Are you afraid that I might ask you for some?"

"No," Sutton replied. "It's just an awkward subject. Some people find it uncomfortable."

"Talking about money doesn't make me uncomfortable," Scooter countered. "Why should it? I don't have any." His tone seemed to indicate that this was an honorable thing.

"Is that by choice?"

"*By choice?*" He rose up on his elbows as he threw back the words.

Sutton stared at him defiantly, braced for an argument and not willing to back down. "You call yourself Scooter and serve up beer for a living. Were you under the impression that you'd make the same salary as a stockbroker doing that?"

"You make me sound like some loser working the beer booth at a fair. I'm a bartender."

"Well, unless you *own* the bar you're tending, I don't think you'll ever be happy with the pay grade."

"Man, you're some kind of snobby bitch. What do *you* do for a living?"

"I'm in television. For years I was a broadcast news journalist, and just re—"

"Never heard of you."

"I think that says more about your general awareness of things than my career profile. You've never heard of *Meet the Press*, either."

"Well, shit, I'm poor and working a dead-end job. Why not label me a dumb ass, too?"

"That's your self-assessment, not mine."

"You know, you're much more fun when you have a cock stuffed in one of your holes."

"I was just thinking the same thing about you," Sutton snapped back.

Scooter jumped out of bed and began retrieving his scattered clothes from the floor. "I guess I should take off. I've done my part volunteering for the elderly."

"You bastard!" Sutton screamed. In the heat of her instant outrage, she grabbed a crystal diamond-shaped paperweight from the nightstand and hurled the heavy object at Scooter. It hit the corner of his forehead, mere millimeters from his eye.

"Jesus Christ! You crazy bitch!"

Sutton, still fuming and not even a little bit sorry for the random act of violence, glared daggers at him. The fucker was only bleeding. For hurling those words, she wanted him dead.

Scooter winced in pain. He touched the wound, then checked his fingertips, which were now dripping blood, too. "Shit!" He looked at her with a mixture of confusion and fear. "What the fuck?"

"Lesson number one, asshole. Never toss out shots about a lady's age."

"It was a joke!"

"But not funny. Obviously."

Scooter shook his head, as if shell-shocked. "Yeah, obviously."

Sutton felt a fleeting moment of regret. It passed. And then just as quickly, it returned. She sighed. "Do you need medical attention?"

Scooter reached down on the floor for his crumpled underwear, then used it to blot dry the injury. "I'll be all right. I don't have insurance anyway."

"Of course not." She draped a blanket around her like a bath towel and crawled out of bed to inspect the damage herself. It was a nasty gash. Stitches would make it pretty again. Forgoing them would make him look Steve McQueen tough. "You'll live."

Scooter rolled his eyes. "Look, everybody, it's Florence Nightingale."

She cracked a smile. "A historical reference that predates Britney Spears? I'm impressed."

Scooter managed a crooked smile. "I didn't really mean what I said. I was just talking shit. I had fun last night. This morning, too. You're a great fuck."

Sutton kissed him full on the lips. "Now that's what a woman likes to hear."

"See, I'm not so dumb."

She took another glance at the wound and began to worry. "You probably need to get that checked."

Scooter strutted into the bathroom to see for himself. He returned with a diffident shrug. "I'll be fine. It's not worth half a day waiting in the emergency room."

Suddenly, Sutton felt an inexplicable urge to baby him. "Are you sure? It's really an ugly cut."

"I'm tough. I watched as they stuck a needle through my dick. And I never flinched once."

Sutton took possession of the bloody underwear in his hand and gently wiped the wound. Now that the bleeding had stopped, it looked less severe.

"What happened here exactly?" Scooter asked. "I've heard of road rage. Was that . . . I don't know . . . age rage?"

"Something like that." With exaggerated shame, Sutton bit down on her lower lip. But then she narrowed her eyes. "It was a really mean thing to say, though. You're lucky I don't keep a gun in the nightstand drawer."

"Yeah, lucky me," Scooter deadpanned.

"Even so, I want to do something to make it up to you."

He shook his head. "Forget about it."

"No, I insist." An idea came to mind. "We could go shopping."

Scooter's eyebrows shot up. "For a mattress?"

"For something that fits inside a gift bag," Sutton countered.

Scooter thought about it. "My roommate gave away my Xbox to score some drugs."

Sutton nodded. "Okay. Buying you a shirt sounds sexier, but you're the one who's bleeding. Xbox it is."

THE IT PARADE
BY JINX WIATT

Fill in the Blanks

Children, behave! Ex-boyfriends (both those from the past and those soon-to-be) can bring out the absolute worst in girls . . . and boys. It took more than a burly bouncer to control the mania and mayhem at New York's tough door haunt for rock lovers. A trusted source tells me there were slaps, curses, threats, tears, and at least one secret video. But that's what comes out of the kitchen when you mix up America's prince, his heiress wife, his TV-star ex, comedy's number one female scribe, the new Carson Kressley, and that notorious queer who loves to pass himself off as a celeb relative or fake royal.

14

Emma

There were three fast knocks on her dressing room door. "It's Jay, Emma. Are you decent?"

"Depends on who you ask."

He slipped inside and gave her a supportive smile. "Oh, the vagaries of fame."

Emma rolled her eyes. "More like the insanity of others." She was fully made up, perfectly coiffed, well-prepped for the segments ahead, and ready to get today's goddamn show over with.

"Some new viewer research is in," Jay announced. "Do you have a minute?"

Emma glanced at the digital clock. "I have seven, actually."

"They like you," Jay said. "They really, really like you." One beat. "I'm talking about the viewers."

"That's why I got the job," Emma remarked easily. "I have a high Q rating. Among the eighteen to fifty-four demographic. Not the regulars at Retox in Chelsea. They don't like me at all there."

Jay pulled a face. "Please don't become my Shannen Doherty. I don't need a Shannen Doherty. Or a Lindsay Lohan for that matter."

Emma sighed wearily. "Honestly, Jay, I'm not sure how much serious news girl is left in me anymore. But there's at least enough to prevent that. Promise."

Jay put his hands together in prayer. "Bless you, my child. I would ask what happened over the weekend, but I'm guessing it would take you longer than seven minutes to tell me."

Emma glanced at the clock again. "Actually, it's down to five now. Talk fast. We'll get coffee later, and I'll fill you in on the drama."

He nodded eagerly and perched himself on the edge of the sofa. "It's a date. Viewers are responding to you in a big way. They want to be you. You're their aspirational host."

"They want to *be* me?" Emma asked warily. "Our viewers must be dumb."

"They want Finn to be their best friend," Jay went on.

"Our viewers must be very dumb."

"They want to see Simone's personal wardrobe closet."

"Our viewers must be shallow and bored."

"And they want to see more of Mio and Mako Kometani."

"Our viewers must be idiots."

Jay shrugged. "What can I say? It's daytime."

Emma laughed.

"I didn't mean that. If this conversation ends up on You-Tube, then we are both fired." He made a show out of looking around for a hidden camera.

"You didn't mention Sutton," Emma said.

"Her research didn't spike."

Emma raised a brow.

"Don't get me wrong," Jay said quickly. "It wasn't negative. Viewers see her as a stabilizer. She's a welcome mature presence. But in this latest research it was the younger personalities that generated the most feedback."

Emma nodded. "No matter what it says, trust me, Jay.

Viewers do not want to be me. Who should I slip that note to?"

"We've made ratings gains with each successive airing," Jay said. "Viewers are responding to you. *Seriously*. Anyway, that's just the little bit of sunshine I wanted to spread. I actually came in here to ask you about something else."

Emma gazed at him expectantly.

"White Glove is already thinking about possible brand extensions of the program. Do you think Garrison would be willing to discuss the possibility of a magalog?"

Emma was stunned. "For *The Beehive*?"

Jay nodded. "The editorial package is already there—career advice from you, humor pieces and trend analysis from Finn, fashion obsessions from Simone, and sage advice on life and living from Sutton."

"God, everything is happening so fast," Emma murmured, still trying to wrap her head around the concept but knowing in her gut that it was a slam dunk. "Okay, sure, I'll talk to him."

"Thanks. And you're right—it is happening fast. So strap yourself in tight. My hunch is that you, Finn, and Simone are going to get the *Queer Eye for the Straight Guy* treatment. When that show hit, a world of opportunity opened up for each of those guys. That can be quite the tightwire act, too. You have to strike while the interest is red hot but at the same time be very smart about your choices."

Emma got hung up on the concept of *smart choices*. If only she had made one of those Saturday night and stayed at Delilah's apartment instead of insisting that they go out. She would have never darkened the doorway of Retox. And she would have never seen Dean Paul dancing with that Blondie wannabe . . .

★ ★ ★

She was total bar trash, bleached from her roots to her split ends and wearing a white sequined top cut down to there over a pair of black leggings and thigh-high vinyl boots.

Dean Paul Lockhart was grinding against her with the kind of smile that told the room he considered himself a shoo-in for the next season of *Dancing with the Stars*.

Emma retreated quickly. One of those Horny Goat drinks turned to two. Then three.

"No more!" Delilah had intervened when she wanted a fourth. "Switch to water."

"It's too late for that," Emma slurred. "And I'm already too far gone."

"You have a point," Delilah agreed. She drank up and motioned for two more.

"He's a pig," Emma grumbled. "Actually, he's worse than a pig." One beat. "What's worse than a pig?"

"Dean Paul is," Delilah said. "I happen to like pigs. George Clooney had a pig. His name was Max. He slept with George. I wish I could've been a pig named Max."

"Me, too," Emma murmured. She glanced back at the dance floor she was trying so hard to ignore.

Dean Paul was moving his hips in perfect synchronization to Lenny Kravitz's guitar riffs from "Lady." And Debbie Harry's slutty niece was enjoying every raunchy moment of the lusty action.

Emma spun back around, feeling a powerful flush of the most regrettable kind of anger—drunken anger. "He's vile," she seethed.

"So is she," Delilah put in. "I feel like I should take a cycle of antibiotics just for watching her from this distance."

Emma stewed over the past in the way that only too much alcohol could make you do. "If he had married me instead of Tilly, then this would still be happening. Only I'd be the one at home with our baby. And he'd still be here with that . . . *girl.*"

Delilah leveled a serious look at Emma. "You're exactly right. Men like Dean Paul never change. Unless they're Warren Beatty. And who really cares if a man makes that change at the age of sixty? He stops running around just in time for you to deal with his gout and his back problems? Fuck that."

Emma raised her Horny Goat in salute. "Yeah, fuck that!"

"Fuck what exactly? Who knows? I might actually want to."

Emma turned to her left to identify the owner of that voice and came face-to-face with her favorite cohost. "Oh, Finn!" she exclaimed delightfully, wrapping her arms around him. "I'm so happy to see you! Have you met Delilah?"

He extended his hand. "Not formally, but I TiVo *Laugh Track* every week. I love your work."

"Thank you. I wish more of it made it onto the air, but what can you do when you're the only female writer in a room full of Harvard grads?"

"I'll never get that. Funny is funny. What does gender have to do with it?"

"Unfortunately, I exist in a world where the first person who throws up after the deviled egg eating contest gets the biggest laugh."

"Poor you," Finn said sympathetically.

Delilah regarded him strangely for a moment. "I'm not trying to stereotype. But is this really your kind of place?"

"First of all, you *are* stereotyping," Finn accused lightly. "And, no, it's not my kind of place. I'm here on a rescue operation."

"I need rescuing," Emma put in desperately. "Take me anywhere else. *Please.*"

"Someone's got a cell phone video of Dean Paul dancing with that—"

"Whore," Emma finished.

"As I understand it, her name's Juicy," Finn said. "But I'm sure that she also answers to Whore."

"How do you know this?" Delilah asked.

"That she also answers to Whore? I've seen her eye makeup." Emma nearly doubled over with laughter.

"No," Delilah clarified. "How do you know about this cell phone video?"

Finn sighed heavily. "It's a long story. I know the guy who has it. He's a hanger-on of the worst kind. I'm hoping I can convince him to—"

"Not bury it!" Emma protested hotly. "Let the creep sell it to TMZ or do whatever he wants to do. Dean Paul deserves that!"

Finn looked at Emma, then over to Delilah. "How much?"

"Three bottles of wine at my apartment and four Horny Goats," she answered.

Finn focused on Emma. "Dean Paul might deserve it, but Tilly doesn't . . . well, actually, Tilly deserves it, too. *Cantaloupe.* The innocent baby. She's the one who doesn't deserve it. The *only* one, apparently. Her parents' marriage may be hanging on by a tattered thread, but the snap doesn't need to come from something like this."

Emma felt a surge of irrational hostility. "You're just protecting Dean Paul because you're in love with him!" she sneered.

"I love him," Finn said matter-of-factly. "As a friend. I'm not *in* love with him."

Emma stumbled and splayed out her hands in some grand theatrical gesture. "Ladies and gentlemen, please welcome, Finn Robards, Queen of Denial!" She cackled at her own bitter play on words.

Finn's face turned pink with embarrassment. "Somebody take this drunk bitch home," he said to no one in particular.

"I'll be more than happy to."

Growing increasingly bleary-eyed, Emma spun around to see a glowering Tilly Lockhart.

"I assume you live at the bottom of the Hudson River?" Tilly continued.

Finn stepped forward to intercede. "Tilly, wait—"

"Wait a minute!" Emma fumed. "Who the hell do you think you are?"

"Mrs. Dean Paul Lockhart. The woman you wish you were. I came to take my husband home. I hear he's been dirty dancing with a trashy blonde. Are you done with him yet?"

Emma made a fast move toward Tilly.

But Delilah moved faster to hold her back. Then she stepped in front to directly address Tilly. "You have made three terrible mistakes. The first one was marrying that overrated playboy. The second one was naming your child after a melon. And the third one was tonight's case of mistaken identity. Follow my finger." Delilah pointed to Juicy and Dean Paul practically dry-humping each other against the speaker in the corner.

Tilly gasped in horror.

Emma took the opportunity to fling what remained of her Horny Goat into Tilly's face. But in her drunken clumsiness, she missed and sloshed an innocent bystander.

And that's the last thing she remembered before waking up on Delilah's couch the next morning with the worst hangover of her life.

"Ninety seconds, Ms. Ronson!" The production assistant's voice sent her careening back to the awful present, where things were messier than ever.

THE IT PARADE
BY JINX WIATT

Fill in the Blanks

Who ever would've thought that the busiest bee on that much buzzed about new daytime chat fest would turn out to be the poor little rich boy? He's quite the character, and I have it on good authority that he was born with a silver spoon in his . . . ahem . . . *mouth*. Okay, I'll be nice. Stories are circulating that in addition to his television hosting duties, this ambitious lad might open up his own Manhattan gathering spot for the beautiful, the rich, and, of course, the badly behaved. From dilettante to workaholic? Must be something in the honey, darlings.

15
Finn

"Ladies and gentlemen, you have officially entered *The Beehive!*"
the announcer boomed. "Please welcome your hosts . . . Sutton
Lancaster . . . Emma Ronson . . . Simone Williams . . . and Finn
Robards!"

As they emerged from the backstage holding area, thunderous applause greeted them. The instant adrenaline from
the reaction shifted Finn's toxic state of mind from I-hate-
these-bitches to let's-give-the-people-the-best-show-we-can.

"Thank you . . . thank you," Emma said, pushing down
her manicured hands in a gracious gesture to bring an end to
the ovation. "Welcome back to *The Beehive*. It's Monday. And
I think it's safe to say that all of us here had an eventful weekend."

"Oh, really? Why do you say that?" Finn remarked. The
studio crowd seemed to pick up on his fake innocence and
real bitchiness. They tittered uncomfortably.

"I might've read a few things . . . *experienced* a few things,"
Emma admitted with a certain self-deprecating charm. "Seriously, though, my weekend was awful."

"Mine sucked," Finn added.

"Mine started off terrible but ended well," Simone put in.

Sutton just sat there, a somewhat vacant smile glazed across her face. For the first time, Finn noticed her new (and not necessarily improved) look. Edgier eye makeup, hair tousled for that just-out-of-bed impact, a much shorter skirt, and loads of rock-inspired costume jewelry, some of it sporting skull-and-crossbones charms.

"And your weekend, *madam*?" Finn pressed. "How was it?"

Sutton gave him a pointed look. "Exhausting."

"Yes," Finn said with a cheeky knowingness. "As I remember, men that age typically are."

The audience hooted and whistled.

Sutton pursed her lips disapprovingly, but her mouth still betrayed a hint of a smile. "I believe it's time for 'Bee in Our Bonnet.'"

The crowd erupted at the mere mention of the popular segment. Its accompanying logo flashed onto the giant monitor.

"Because of the wonderful people in this audience—and all of the wonderful viewers watching at home—our show has become an amazing success," Sutton said. "With that comes a certain degree of media interest and scrutiny that we just have to deal—"

"Honey, you are being way too diplomatic about this," Finn cut in. "Allow me." He turned to face the studio crowd. "Gossip columnist Jinx Wiatt is on the show today to plug her new book, and if all of you would just politely turn away and cover your ears, then the four of us will each take a turn strangling the bitch."

The audience howled.

"That's *exactly* where I was heading. If you had only given me a chance!" Sutton replied, earning a few laughs of her own.

"Does everybody read *The It Parade*?" Emma inquired.

The explosion of applause provided the answer.

"I have it bookmarked," Simone admitted. "It's one of the first sites I go to in the morning . . . *after* I get my grande-triple-hazelnut-sugar-free-nonfat latte from Starbucks. Because before I get that, I am *impossible*. Anyway, I was reading it the other day, and I'm, like, 'Oh my God, who is that? I feel like I know her.' And then I realized that I *was* her."

Emma nodded with bemused empathy. "For those of you who don't read this stuff . . . well, first of all, congratulations! You're probably too busy surfing serious news sites—"

"Are there serious news sites online?" Finn interrupted. "I must have the wrong Internet."

Another big laugh from the crowd.

"There's a whole world out there, Finn," Emma dead-panned. "It goes beyond *The It Parade*, eBay, and porn."

Finn let her get the laugh and get away with the line. After all, it was nothing that he had not—or would not—say about himself.

"Seriously," Emma went on, "for those of you who don't know, *The It Parade* is a popular online gossip column that never mentions actual names, but the clues are so obvious that identifying the subjects becomes a fairly easy game. Also, there's a viral quality to it, because the columns get forwarded in e-mails and then the bloggers get started with their two cents." She let out a frustrated sigh. "Pretty soon your mother is calling to ask if you really *are* still upset about your last breakup."

"Would the column get half the attention if real names were used?" Simone wondered aloud. "I mean, think about it. 'Simone Williams tried to shop at Christian Dior, but her credit card was declined.' *There*. A quick and dirty bit of gossip. Over and done with. But without a name, it takes on another life cycle, not to mention endless speculation. By the end of the day, I'm giving my building super oral favors to make the rent. Ridiculous!"

"I can barely get a lightbulb changed for doing that," Finn cracked. "I need to move into your building."

This time even his cohosts joined in on the cacophonous laughter.

"We'll be right back after the break . . . with Jinx Wiatt," Emma said, beaming a perfect stage girl smile. "Don't go anywhere!"

As was the custom during the first commercial interlude, Finn and Simone ventured out to interact with audience members while Emma studied her notes for the upcoming segments and Sutton engaged in a hushed conference with Jay.

The minutes ticked by like seconds. Suddenly, they were reassembled at the table.

"She's one of the country's most widely read gossip scribes," Emma began. "And now she can add bestselling author to her résumé with the immediate success of her first book, *Ex Marks the Spot: How to Know When You're Really Over Him.* Please welcome to *The Beehive* . . . Jinx Wiatt!"

The infamous vixen came strutting out in a towering pair of Manolo Blahniks. But she barely passed the five-foot mark. This girl was very tiny, very tan, very blonde, and, judging from the enormous princess–cut yellow diamond adorning her most significant finger, very well taken care of. After a flurry of double air kisses to each host, Jinx settled into her assigned spot in the middle of the group. "My ears are burning!" she enthused in a voice that reeked of girlishness.

"Just burning?" Sutton remarked. "They probably should be bleeding."

Jinx giggled.

Simone jumped in without preamble. "Where do you get your information? Do you have, like, spies *everywhere*?"

Jinx waved off the thought in a way that managed to emphasize her yellow diamond. "Oh, it's not that sinister. I go here. I go there. Sources call me." She beamed a megawatt smile. "I think people end up sharing more with me, because I don't name names. I'm a firm believer in protecting the guilty." She punctuated her last line with an outrageous giggle.

Sutton just sat there, stone-faced. "Do you actually find it rewarding to traffic in other people's miseries this way?"

Jinx's smile froze. There was a steel-like glint to her eyes that told Finn she had come under attack countless times . . . and always emerged unscathed. "It's not all misery," she countered. "For instance, I recently reported about an older talk show host who slipped into the restroom at a bar with a much younger man and stayed there for twenty minutes or more. As the story was told to me, they both left looking quite happy."

Sutton's eyes narrowed into hateful slits.

Finn moved fast to intercede. "Your column often goes beyond the reporting of gossipy tidbits and seems to take aim at people's emotional lives."

"I have a background in psychology," Jinx explained. "So that's only natural."

"But is it responsible?" Emma asked. "As you've explained, much of your information comes to you from random sources—"

"Never random," Jinx argued. "My sources are vetted for accuracy. I stand behind every column I write one hundred percent, and if there's ever so much as a shred of doubt about the veracity of a story, then I back off until I'm certain. It's the only standard to live by."

"Yes," Sutton said haughtily. "You have such high journalistic principles. A regular Woodward and Bernstein."

"I do consider myself a journalist," Jinx said archly.

Finn saw an opening to kill. "I once had a friend who considered himself Steven Spielberg's nephew. Now he has outstanding arrest warrants in two states."

The audience laughed uproariously.

But Jinx could not be rattled. "Interestingly, it's not the alleged inaccuracies that cause discomfort to the subjects of my columns." She paused a beat and fixed a meaningful stare on Finn. "It's the deeper truths. People tend to live in denial."

Finn knew that Jinx stood ready to play armchair psychotherapist on the subject of his friendship with Dean Paul. But there was a time to throw down, and there was a time to retreat. Finn chose the latter.

"Tell us about your book," Simone said, holding up a copy of *Ex Marks the Spot: How to Know When You're Really Over Him.* "How did that come about?"

"I'm famous within my friendship clique for staging elaborate female summits," Jinx gushed. "I plan them for big stage of life changes like engagements, first pregnancies, divorces, career reinventions—anything that's huge and life altering. And what I've observed is that the ex factor—I'm talking the significant ex here—really does mark the spot in terms of how women perceive themselves and embrace new opportunities." She glanced over at Finn. "And some men as well. It works both ways."

Emma jumped in. "One of your recommendations for getting over an ex is something you call 'Closure Sex.'"

Jinx nodded. "That's when you sleep with him one last time. Go out with a bang. Literally."

The crowd broke into titters.

"Too many women over-romanticize the last time they were intimate with an ex," Jinx went on. "I'm all for a dirty round of sex to say good-bye and good riddance. It's empowering. And it will leave him second-guessing letting you go, which is another plus." She winked.

"Well, what if your ex is a stalker?" Simone asked. "I'm speaking hypothetically, of course." She rolled her eyes and made an adorable, who-am-I-kidding face that amused the audience. "But I would think sleeping with your stalker ex could be . . . I don't know . . . a sign of encouragement you might not want to send."

"Stalking is such an overused term," Jinx said. "It rarely applies. I find that many self-proclaimed stalker victims are simply not ready to let go of the relationship, either. They're holding on just as hard."

Simone let out an audible gasp. "Well, that may be true in some cases—"

"But not yours," Jinx finished in a patronizing tone. "It never is."

Simone turned to address the audience, as if convincing them were the only way to get through this now. "My ex-boyfriend kidnapped my cat!"

There was a collective moan of astonished sympathy.

Jinx raised a hand to silence the crowd. "Wait a minute. Did he grow attached to this animal during your time together?"

"Well . . . I . . . I guess," Simone stammered. "But the cat is *mine!*"

Triumphantly, Jinx tilted her head to the side. "It's not uncommon for people to withhold visitation with pets and children. Ostensibly, it's to punish the ex. But it only serves to ratchet up the conflict, which keeps the connection alive, even if that connection is negative."

Simone just sat there in stunned silence.

"The little games we play to convince ourselves that we're over our exes are endless," Jinx went on. "The cougar phenomenon is a perfect example. A man leaves a woman for a younger girl. So what does that woman do? She goes out to find a younger man to prove that she's still vital."

"But men have been doing that for years!" Sutton protested hotly.

Halfway into the rebuke, Jinx began to shake her head. "Men do it for sex. Not because they were dumped or feeling less desirable or anything else. It's just for the sex, sex, and more sex."

"So you're saying a woman can't be motivated by the same physical need," Sutton challenged.

"I didn't say that explicitly," Jinx argued. "I believe a woman can be motivated by sex. No doubt. But the predicating factor is almost always something else. We're complicated creatures that way."

Finn threw himself into the middle of the melee. "You've positioned yourself as the Jedi Master of thriving after a breakup. What kind of training do you have?"

Jinx gave him a shrewd smile. "I've been through my fair share of breakups, if that's what you're asking."

"That's precisely what I'm asking," Finn said.

"It took many breakups to develop the insight to write this book," Jinx admitted. "Many *bad* breakups."

"Anyone we might know?" Finn inquired.

"As a matter of fact, yes," Jinx said silkily. "But I'll never say who." She zeroed in on Emma. "Ms. Ronson, you're uncharacteristically quiet. Has this subject touched a nerve?"

Like a cat sensing danger, Emma lengthened her spine. "I'm just curious. And I'm sure our viewers are as well. What would you say are the telltale signs of being over an ex?"

Jinx appeared to savor the question. "The surest sign is to see him with someone else and not feel . . . *tortured*. That must be particularly difficult in your case. I imagine the intense media coverage of Dean Paul Lockharts's romance with Tilly Winston came at a time when you were still reeling."

Finn saw Emma's face turn ashen. In a pathetic way, he could relate. Hearing Benji speak of Dean Paul's dalliance with the rock chick blonde had done quite a number on him. And seeing it happen with his very own eyes had done yet another.

Don't be jealous. Who knows? Next time I cheat, maybe it'll be with you.

The words were typical Dean Paul. He often talked smack without consideration for the potential impact. It had been a stupid joke, unintentionally cruel teasing, a flirtatious way to acknowledge that he knew about Finn's secret desires. And until last night, Finn had not realized how much he was truly longing for the fantasy to come true.

"That explains your career change," Jinx was saying to Emma. "Women in the throes of a painful break will often do something drastic—change jobs, change their look—in the false hope that the external shake-up will somehow calm the internal feelings. But it rarely does. There's always the relief that distraction brings, but when the lights go down at night, there's no escaping the yearning for an ex."

"Okay," Emma snapped. "I get it. We're all hopelessly hung up on our exes and living in a constant state of delusion to think otherwise. Now that we've established that, tell me why anyone should go out and spend twenty-five dollars on your book."

"There *are* some painful chapters to get through," Jinx admitted. "But that's important self-assessment work that has to be done. It's the only way to grow." She smiled a condescending smile. "There's also a complete guide to becoming your own girlfriend. If every woman would do that for herself, then the world would be a much happier place."

"*Finding the Girlfriend Within?*" Finn asked in a mocking tone.

"Exactly," Jinx said, giving him an upbeat nod.

Suddenly, Finn was filled with a glorious sense of come-uppance, not only for himself, but for Sutton, Emma, and Simone, too. "Aren't you treading on old Brad Good terri-tory?"

Jinx gave him a blank look.

"Years ago he gave that same spiel to gay men with a sappy little tome called *Finding the Boyfriend Within*."

Jinx shifted in her seat. "I've never heard of it," she said tightly. "Or this Brad Good person for that matter."

Finn shot back a devilish smirk. "How . . . *convenient*."

"In this case, yes," Jinx countered. "And as you well know, the truth can also be *inconvenient*."

Sutton recognized her opportunity and pounced. "So is this an original work, or did you lift an idea from a gay writer and package it for a straight audience?"

Jinx was visibly offended. "I did not *lift* any idea from any-one. Like I said, I've never even heard of this gay book. And by the way, Avril Lavigne called. She wants her jewelry back."

The studio audience rumbled with boos, hisses, and a smattering of laughs.

Emma seized control. "The author is Jinx Wiatt. The book is *Ex Marks the Spot: How to Know When You're Really Over Him*. The baggage is something we all carry. Please stay with us. We'll be back after a short break with more from *The Beehive*."

Jinx waited for the on-camera light to change, then stormed off the set without a word.

"I think she likes Regis and Kelly better," Finn remarked.

Nervously, Simone bit down on her lower lip. "It was bad enough before. What's she going to write about us now?"

"Who gives a shit?" Sutton spat. "The bitch deserved it.

And we're still the walking wounded. I'd hardly call what happened unfair."

Finn slipped out of his chair and started toward the backstage area that led to his dressing room. He rarely needed a drink in the middle of a show. But he needed one now.

Emma followed in hot pursuit. "Finn, wait—"

He stopped and spun around.

Emma looked stricken with regret. "About Saturday night . . . I owe you an apology. I was drunk. I didn't know what I was saying."

"How very Mel Gibson of you."

Emma's smile was pleading. "You have to forgive me. I can't take you being mad at me."

He shrugged off the notion. "Bygones. I've said worse things to people when I was sober."

Emma breathed a sigh of relief and leaned in to embrace him.

"We've got maybe two minutes, and I need a shot of something before we go back on air," Finn whispered into her ear. "Are you game?"

Emma drew back and clutched her stomach. "Oh, God, no. I'm on the second day of a murderous hangover. If you *ever* see me with another Horny Goat in my hand, I hereby grant you permission to shoot me on sight."

Finn laughed a little.

Emma regarded him seriously for a moment. "I might be over-assuming something here when I say this, but . . . it's going to be hard . . . to stay friends with him and not end up getting hurt."

"I know that," Finn admitted quietly. "But I think protecting myself by walking away from the friendship might hurt more."

Emma put a comforting hand on Finn's forearm. "You know, that son of a bitch doesn't deserve half the love that's thrown his way."

Finn managed a half smile. "And yet here we stand pining away for him."

Emma sighed deeply. "How can two smart people be so fucking stupid?"

THE IT PARADE
BY JINX WIATT

Fill in the Blanks

You never really know whether you are over the old ex until you start dating the future ex. That's when the comparisons start. Who's the better kisser? Who's the better lover? Who's funnier? Who actually listens to what you say? That gorgeous Black American Princess may be dodging creditors like sniper fire, but she's also giving the ex rules from my new book a serious workout. Smart girl. If I were a betting woman, I'd put money on the fact that the baseball hunk is no homerun in the sack against hip-hop's hottest mogul.

16
Simone

Simone glared at the vibrating mobile phone. She knew that the incoming number was a creditor. They had become relentless. Reluctantly, she took the call. "Hello?"

"Simone Williams, please." The voice was female and bitchy as hell on the first syllable drop.

"Speaking."

"This is Jean Kent from American Express. I'm calling in reference to your outstanding balance of eleven thousand two hundred thirty-eight dollars and eighteen cents."

Simone's stomach dropped. *Eleven thousand dollars?* "Excuse me, there must be some kind of mistake. My bill couldn't possibly be that high."

"I see no record of any disputed charges."

"But I just paid—"

"Your account is past due by more than sixty days," the woman cut in. "I can take a payment over the phone."

A sick feeling spread across Simone's abdomen as she recalled the creditor paying frenzy that had commenced with her first salaried check from *The Beehive*. Money had gone out to American Express Blue, American Express One, American

Express Optima, and American Express Platinum. "Which card is this?"

"American Express Gold Rewards."

"Oh," Simone said flatly. No money had gone out to that account. *Oops.* Well, who could really blame her? She had so many different cards. As busy as she was, Simone really needed a bookkeeper to sort out everything.

"I can take a payment over the phone right now," the woman pressed.

"Yes, you've made that quite clear," Simone snapped. "But at the moment, I'm not prepared to do that."

"How much can you pay? We're willing to work with you on a scheduled payment plan. Of course, your card privileges will remain suspended until the balance is paid in full."

Nervously, Simone began digging into her leggings. Within seconds, her nails had made a vicious run going from calf to ankle. "I need some time to . . . study my cash flow situation. I'll have to call you back."

"When can we expect to hear from you?"

"Very soon. By the end of the day at the latest."

"I'll note that on the account."

Simone hung up. She took in a deep breath, trying not to panic. *Eleven thousand dollars.* It seemed impossible. Well, not really. She had charged the limited edition super large bottle (twenty heavenly ounces) of Juicy Couture perfume. That alone had been three grand. Now she only had eight thousand to account for.

Part of her problem was her inability to sleep through the night. Sometimes she could just lay there for what seemed like hours, worrying herself sick about Tommy Robb or the state of her personal finances. And then, to soothe her nerves and boost her mood, Simone would find herself shopping online in the wee hours.

Neiman Marcus provided the best therapy. She always paid extra for express shipping and the deluxe gift wrap, even including encouraging notes to herself. Two days later, she was opening a lavish box with a card that read, SIMONE, YOU DESERVE THIS! The only sense of remorse came when the Jean Kents of the world started calling. Sixty days should *not* be considered past due. They should give her a month or so to get around to opening the bill, and after that, at least another two months to arrange proper payment. Under that civilized arrangement, her account would still be in good standing.

Simone gazed at her reflection in the dressing room mirror. She tried to engage herself in deep thought on the perils of reckless spending. But she became preoccupied by the fact that she really needed a Resculpting Facial at Tracy Martyn. There went three hundred dollars. So much for soul-searching.

On a sudden impulse, Simone called her longtime agent, Sue Hotchner. With all the attention surrounding *The Beehive*, there had to be a way to make a fast paycheck.

Sue answered her line with the muffled sound of food in her mouth. "Sue Hotchner."

"Hi, Sue, it's Simone Williams."

"Hold on a sec." There was the sound of more eating, rustling wrappers, and then a hacking smoker's cough. "Sorry about that. How are you, sweetheart? The show is doing great. I'm proud of you."

Simone managed a faint smile. "According to the critics, I'm just along for the ride."

"Fuck 'em," Sue barked. "Your show's a hit. That's all that matters."

"It doesn't pay enough," Simone said matter-of-factly.

Sue fell silent for a moment. "It's too soon to renegotiate, doll. Wait until the show gets picked up for a second season. I'll go to bat for you then."

"I understand that," Simone said. "But I need money now. As fast as possible."

"Are you on drugs?" Sue asked sharply.

"No!" Simone protested fiercely. "I have a sky high American Express bill."

"Oh, well, that's respectable. I can get behind that."

"I need something on the weekends," Simone said. "Or at night. The show has me tied up in the morning and most of the afternoon, so the little acting gigs don't work anymore."

"It just so happens that one of my soap stars fell through on a Target store opening in New Jersey this Saturday. Pays five grand for just a few hours' work."

"I'll take it," Simone blurted without so much as a micro-moment of consideration. After all, five thousand dollars was five thousand dollars.

"They want a hunk, but I think I can sell them on you."

"What do I have to do exactly?" Simone asked.

"Cut the ribbon at the official opening ceremony, pose for pictures, that sort of thing. Let me get it set up. I'll call you back."

Simone nodded proudly, impressed with her industrious, proactive approach to the American Express problem. And then a ripple of awareness flowed through her . . . that the cheese factor for this gig was high. Very high.

A department store opening. *In New Jersey.* Just when she thought true success was within reach, it had come to this. The handlers of Miss Hawaiian Tropic had probably turned it down.

But what else could Simone expect? Lower tier opportunities were the rule—not the exception—at the Sue Hotchner Agency. The best opportunity to come Simone's way in years had been *The Beehive.* And she had stumbled across that on her own during a long wait to audition for Sassy Black Hooker

Number Two on one of the *Law & Order* franchise shows. Sue had worked the phones and somehow wrangled an interview for Simone. But a real agent would have known about the show from the jump.

Sutton and Emma were polished television pros with top-flight agents behind them. Even Finn had managed to score a serious representative at the William Morris Agency. And here was Simone, stuck with a second-stringer like Sue Hotchner, a fat, chain-smoking hustler who worked out of her apartment on the Lower East Side.

Simone's mobile vibrated.

It was Sue. "Hi, doll. It's done. Ribbon cutting is set for ten o'clock. They're thrilled to have you. I'll e-mail the rest of the details."

"Great," Simone murmured, her enthusiasm already down for the count. She knew that by Saturday she would probably prefer waterboarding torture to following through on the appearance.

She began gathering her things to leave and noticed Jinx Wiatt's book on the edge of the end table.

I find that many self-proclaimed stalker victims are simply not ready to let go of the relationship, either. They're holding on just as hard.

As the horrible woman's words ricocheted in her mind, Simone felt a renewed sense of outrage as she stomped over to the sofa and began to flip though the bitch's self-help tripe. She stopped on a section entitled THE RULE OF EX-TREMITIES: SHOCK YOUR EX RIGHT OUT OF YOUR SYSTEM.

ONE SUREFIRE METHOD FOR GETTING OVER AN EX—AND GETTING OVER HIM FAST—IS TO SHOCK YOUR SYSTEM WITH SOME OPPOSITES-

ATTRACT EXCITEMENT. GO TO THE EXTREME, GIRLS. IF YOU BROKE UP WITH A BANKER, THEN START DATING A BANK ROBBER—OR AT LEAST A GUY WHO'S BEEN ARRESTED ONCE. TAKE INVENTORY OF YOUR BEDROOM HABITS, TOO. WHATEVER YOU DIDN'T DO WITH YOUR EX, DEFINITELY DO WITH YOUR NEW MAN. LIGHT BONDAGE, ROLE PLAY, ANAL—UNLESS YOU'VE BEEN A COMPLETE SLUT, THERE HAS TO BE SOMETHING LEFT TO ADD TO YOUR SEXUAL RÉSUMÉ.

Simone tossed the book aside. It was garbage. And the woman who wrote it was toxic waste. The nerve of her to suggest that she was somehow participating in Tommy Robb's madness as a way to stay connected to him. The suggestion was completely ridiculous. She glanced at the book again. *Ex Marks the Spot: How to Know When You're Really Over Him.* What rubbish.

Unable to resist and hating herself for it, Simone began to read more from a section called DON'T FOOL YOURSELF INTO THINKING THAT YOU'RE JUST WAITING FOR SOMEONE EXTRAORDINARY TO COME ALONG.

THE ONLY WAY TO GET OVER AN EX IS TO SADDLE UP AND RIDE AGAIN, EVEN IF THE NEXT GUY TURNS OUT TO BE A TOTAL JERK, TOO. ONE PITFALL OF A NASTY BREAKUP IS TO SIMPLY GIVE UP ON DATING UNTIL YOU MEET MR. FANTASTIC. AND CHANCES ARE YOU'RE WAITING ON A BETTER VERSION OF YOUR EX. IF YOUR GUY WAS A TELEVISION

ACTOR, THEN YOU PROBABLY WANT A MOVIE
STAR. IF HE WAS A CORPORATE EXECUTIVE,
THEN YOU PROBABLY WANT A CEO. AND SO
ON. THE KEY IS DATING, DARLINGS . . . NOT
WAITING. SO IF A CUTE DELIVERY DRIVER ASKS
YOU OUT FOR PIZZA, TELL HIM THAT YOU'LL
BE READY AT SEVEN.

Once again, Simone tossed aside the book in a visible
show of disgust. The trouble was, Jinx Wiatt's chatty prose
seemed to be speaking directly to her situation. A secret part
of Simone was holding out for Derek Jeter, a bigger name in
baseball than Tommy Robb would ever be. And since the
breakup with him, Simone had stopped dating altogether.
Hmm. Maybe she should stop skimming the goddamn book
and just read the stupid thing from cover to cover.

Half-ashamed, she snatched Jinx's ex manifesto and shoved
it inside her Louis Vuitton shopping tote on her way out the
door, realizing with great frustration that she had serious
trouble with men, money, and career. Oh, God! Was *anything*
in Simone's life working?

She waved good-bye to the remaining crew members that
lingered and moved quickly toward the studio exit, anxious
to get back to her apartment to cuddle with Chanel and find
out what financial crimes were waiting in the mailbox.

"Okay, it's on now, bitch!"

Simone glanced up to see an obscenely dressed black
woman rushing toward her on the sidewalk. She froze.

"That's right, high yellow ho! It's on!"

Simone just stood there, observing the scene as if she
were outside her own body. "Excuse me, do I know you?"

"Don't act like you don't know who I am, bitch!"

"This isn't an act," Simone insisted, her fear rising. "I've never seen you before in my life."

"Do you see me now, ho? Do you see me now?"

Simone glanced nervously at passersby, deeply ashamed that even a stranger might assume that she would have any reason to engage in conversation with such a dreadful woman. "You must have me confused with someone else." She started to walk away.

But the woman moved fast to block her. "There's only one high yellow bitch trying to talk to my man." She punctuated her accusation by jabbing her index finger into the center of Simone's chest. "And that's you, ho."

"I have no idea what you're talking about. And please keep your hands off me. God knows where they've been!"

The woman splayed out her hands. "I'll tell you where these hands have been, bitch. I had them wrapped around Kevon's big black dick this morning while I sucked him all the way to heaven and back. *That's* where they've been."

Reeling from shock, Simone gasped. This had to be the most vile woman she had ever encountered.

"And that's where these hands will stay. Believe that, bitch. No high yellow designer-wearing uppity-acting ho is going to move in on my man. Hell to the no. Luscious Brown don't play that shit."

Simone tried to determine which aspect of *Luscious Brown* was worse—the cheap blonde weave, the platinum-enhanced teeth, the breast implants that were at least two sizes too large for her frame, the tight white leather jacket and matching miniskirt, or the freaky nails that extended an inch or more and jingled with little charms attached to the tips. Simone came to the quick conclusion that the entire package was beyond tragic.

"Do you hear me, bitch?" Luscious shouted.

But the worst part about Luscious Brown was not her appearance. It was Simone's realization that she had something in common with her. Polar opposites or not, they both wanted the same thing.

Kevon Edmonds.

THE IT PARADE
BY *JINX WIATT*

Fill in the Blanks

Winners and losers. That's the way
the world keeps score. But a certain
group of randy young bastards who
pride themselves on playing the
cougar game at Stone Rose might
want to consider a recount. According to one chatty member of this little fraternity, every night one lad in
the group draws the short straw and
has to pick up the "cougar with the
oldest tw*#." It rhymes with knot,
darlings, and it's just not a nice word.
In fact, I hate to even repeat it here.
But it turns out the man who lost
came out the real winner in the end.
That aging TV talk show host he seduced and bedded is now his sugar
mommy.

17
Sutton

"How do I look?" Scooter asked.

Sutton adjusted the spread collar on the Italian cotton paisley button-front shirt by Etro. "Absolutely delicious," she whispered, running her hands across his impressive pectorals.

"A woman's never bought me clothes before."

"How does it feel?"

"Kind of hot." He smiled at her.

She smiled back.

The Barney's sales associate hovered. "It's a beautiful shirt. Very classic."

"Do you like it?" Sutton asked.

Scooter strutted over to the full-length mirror and gave himself an approving nod. "I do. I think it suits me."

Sutton slipped a credit card to the associate. "We'll take it."

Scooter noticed a sales tag dangling from the shirt cuff and inspected it curiously. His eyes went wide. "Jesus! This shirt is over three hundred dollars!"

Sutton laughed, then sotto voce to the sales associate murmured, "He's used to shopping at Old Navy."

Scooter disappeared into the fitting room and returned

wearing his own cheap long-sleeve thermal, delicately handling the designer garment by the collar.

The associate stepped forward to take possession. "We just got in some amazing new jeans by Roberto Cavalli that would look great with this. You look like a thirty-two. Am I right?"

Scooter looked at Sutton, a question in his eyes.

She grinned. "Try them on."

The associate needed no further prompting. In record time he was back and ushering Scooter into the fitting room again.

He emerged wearing medium-blue wash jeans with snakeskin-lined pockets. They were just snug enough, clinging to his drum-tight ass as if the denim's life depended on it.

"How do they feel?" Sutton asked.

"Awesome," Scooter said. Once more, he stole a peek at the sales tag. "Holy shit! These cost six hundred bucks!"

Sutton stepped toward him and slipped a hand underneath the waistband. "If you want them, they're yours."

Scooter glanced over to the associate. "Excuse us for a moment. We need to have a short conference." And then he took Sutton by the hand and pulled her inside the tiny fitting room.

Taken by surprise, she started to laugh. "What are you doing?"

Scooter cradled her hips with his hands and moved in close enough to breathe her breath. "You don't have to do this."

"Do what?"

"Buy me expensive things."

"Maybe I want to."

He gave her a sexy, lopsided grin and pressed into her. "It sort of makes me feel like a gigolo."

Sutton could feel his arousal through the top-grade denim. An insatiable need to have him—right here, right now—rose up within her.

Scooter leaned in and gently bit down on her lower lip as his hands slid south to cup her ass. "Do I fuck you that good? So good that you're willing to pay for it?" He pulled her closer against him.

Sutton got drunk on the power and heat of his hardness. An insane, all-consuming desire left her speechless, almost breathless.

"Answer me," Scooter demanded thickly. "Do I fuck you that good?"

Sutton swallowed hard. "Yes." She had no idea what was going to happen next. But she knew with every advancing heartbeat that it would be exquisitely dirty.

In a surprise move, he turned her around, pressed her against the wall, and pushed up her skirt, handling her with deliberate firmness, just a few degrees away from being rough. She could sense his fingers working on the buttons of the Cavalli fly.

He whispered into her ear, "Have you ever done it like this before?"

Sutton shook her head. She was ashamed and turned on at the same time. All that she yearned for was him inside her. It was a raw, naked need.

Scooter shoved two fingers inside her open mouth.

Greedily, Sutton sucked on them as she savored the heat of his hard cock against her.

"Do I fuck you good enough for a new pair of leather boots?"

Sutton nodded, desperate for him to enter her.

Scooter's hot hands pulled at her panties, providing an opening. "Do I fuck you good enough for a Rolex?"

Sutton nodded again.

And then in one vicious thrust, Scooter knocked out what little breath remained in Sutton's lungs. He was fast, ruthless, and selfish. In fact, when he climaxed only a few minutes later, he withdrew and immediately began to get dressed, offering no regard for her pleasure.

For a long moment, she stood there, trying to recover. There was the stark realization that he had just used her body. And there was the more surprising one that she had secretly enjoyed it, orgasm or not. Being a receptacle for his lust filled Sutton with a near-delirious sense of pride. She thought of those stupid executives at the Fox News Channel and their secret memo about the "fuckability factor" of on-air female talent. She had ranked the lowest. If only they could see her now.

"You really are a nasty girl, aren't you? First a blow job in the bathroom at the bar and now a quickie right here. I just might have to finger-fuck you in the cab on the way back to your apartment."

Sutton tried to suppress her reaction, but a little smile of pleasure crept its way onto her mouth.

"Is everything okay?" the associate inquired with a cocked eyebrow as they reemerged onto the sales floor.

"Everything's awesome," Scooter said, tossing him the Cavalli jeans. "We'll take these, too." Suddenly, his eyes wandered, zeroing in on a drop-dead attractive associate strutting toward them.

"If you're looking for something casual, Mr. Friedberg, then these shirts by Etro would be a great choice. They're very popular. Perfect for a night out to a party or a club."

Sutton's stomach did a couple of revolutions as she saw Garrison trundle behind the stick-thin blonde.

He gave the line up of vibrantly printed shirts a derisive snort. "Looks like something a fag would wear."

Then he noticed Sutton and shrewdly looked at Scooter,

the male associate, and back to her again, putting it all together. The man missed no small detail.

"Hello, Garrison," Sutton managed to say. She knew that her face was scarlet. And that it had nothing to do with the fitting room sex.

Garrison nodded. "Sutton. Good to see you." Another glance at Scooter. "Shopping for new school clothes?" He smirked at his own remark.

"Something like that," Sutton replied easily. "You might want to think about enrolling. A man his age could definitely teach you a few things. Hopefully, you're not above learning at this stage in your life."

The rejoinder rattled Garrison's colossal male ego. His angry eyes revealed the impact.

"I'm heading over to shoes," Scooter announced, not bothering to introduce himself, socially inept in the way that so many people born after the Internet was invented seemed to be.

Sutton watched him go, then turned back to face Garrison. This was the first time she had encountered him since receiving the terse breakup letter via FedEx.

"Are you into skateboarders now?" Garrison asked.

"He's a bartender."

"That makes more sense."

"Why?"

"I'm sure being a pro about booze comes in handy." One beat. "For him."

"You son of a bitch," Sutton hissed. "You broke up with me and started dating a girl young enough to be your daughter. Now you're judging *my* behavior?"

"It's different for men. Seeking out the company of younger women is a natural thing for us. We don't look ridiculous doing it."

Sutton laughed in his face. "Buy one of these shirts this twit is trying to sell you, and say that again with a straight face."

The salesgirl glared viciously.

"I just hope she didn't sell you that skirt," Garrison chortled. "Because it looks like she cheated you out of half of it."

Self-consciously, Sutton tugged down on the short hem, as if doing so could make any difference to the daring length.

"Give us a minute," Garrison told the salesgirl, who retreated with obvious relief. He regarded Sutton carefully, almost pitifully. "What are you doing with that loser? Why are you embarrassing yourself like this?"

Sutton hated him. He could be such a mean bastard. "Do you ask yourself those questions whenever you step out the door with *Emma*?"

"I don't have to. She's an accomplished woman."

"So we wouldn't be having this conversation if I happened to be with a twenty-four year-old lawyer?"

Garrison shrugged.

Sutton beamed back a look of disgust. "I don't have to stand here and defend myself against your double standard bullshit."

"Well, don't let me keep you. Go buy your stepson some new sneakers. He's waiting for you in the shoe department, as I understand it."

"Fuck you, Garrison!" The last comment lit an instant fuse, and now Sutton regretted letting her anger show. It was a sure sign of weakness.

So weak that Garrison gave her a wounded look for having hurt her. "Come on, Sutton. Let's not do this. We might both be dating kids, but we're supposed to be the grown-ups."

She took in a deep breath to calm her nerves.

"Besides, we might be working together soon. All of us."

She gave him a strange look. "What do you mean?"

"Emma tells me that they want to do a magalog for *The Beehive*."

Sutton could almost feel her blood begin to boil. "This is the first I've heard of it."

"It's still in the early talking stage," Garrison explained easily. "We're trying to set up an initial meeting with Jay."

"*I'm* the creative consultant for the show!" Sutton raged. "Emma is just air talent!"

"Calm down," Garrison said, his tone oozing patronization. "She just passed along the word that they wanted to have a conversation."

Sutton left Garrison standing there and stalked away, growing increasingly angry with every step. She made a beeline for the exit and hailed a cab. Scooter could buy his own goddamn leather boots. And if he wanted to fuck that idiot salesgirl, then he could do that, too.

The only thing on Sutton's mind was getting rid of Emma Ronson, because *The Beehive* was no longer big enough for both of them.

THE IT PARADE
BY JINX WIATT

Fill in the Blanks

Xs and Os are a flirty way to close personal correspondence. Exes and Ohs! are another situation entirely. Anyone who thought the battle of the blondes (one's a model heiress and married—by a thread these days—to one of America's dreamiest guys, the other's a star-on-the-rise host of one of television's hottest new chat shows) was limited to that drunken dust-up in a Chelsea rock club better think again. These two hellcats have only just begun.

18

Emma

"I'm never drinking again."

Delilah gave Emma an amused glance. "Whatever you say, Tara Reid."

Emma laughed and put her face in her hands. "Oh, what a *horrible* comparison!"

"At least you didn't question the Holocaust," Delilah reasoned. "As far as drunken binges go, it's one you can recover from."

They were huddled over comforting dishes of sheep's ricotta gnudi at the Spotted Pig, an intimate little pub and eatery near Delilah's Greenwich Village apartment.

Emma looked at her friend's wine goblet, then back at her own water glass. "Well . . . maybe just one."

"So much for willpower."

Emma flagged down the waiter for a single serving of the house merlot. "Can I just say one thing?"

Delilah gave her a savage look. "You *promised.*"

"I know," Emma said shamefully. "But—"

"You *promised* that if we went out to dinner, we wouldn't talk about him. Not one word. Not even one syllable."

"You're right. I'm sorry." Silently, Emma toyed with her pasta.

Within moments, Delilah caved in. "Oh, *fine*. What aspect of Dean Paul would you like to deconstruct now?"

Emma gave her a grateful smile. "I have to get this off my chest."

Delilah drank up and wearily waved her on.

"What Tilly said the other night has really been bothering me."

"The part about you being a trashy blonde? Don't let it get to you."

"*No*," Emma said, rolling her eyes. "The part about me wanting to be Mrs. Dean Paul Lockhart. How can I still want that? After everything he's done—to me, to other women, even to her. The way he was carrying on with—"

"Juicy," Delilah cut in. "I believe the young lady's name was Juicy."

"Whatever. It was a disgusting sight," Emma said. "And yet . . ."

"You think you can change him," Delilah finished for her.

The merlot arrived just in the nick of time. Emma indulged with a generous sip. "Yes, I think I can. I think I could be the one."

"You're an idiot. You realize that, don't you?"

Emma nodded, then drained the rest of her wine and motioned for another glass. "Yes, I do."

Delilah pulled a face. "Think about it. I mean, *really* think about it. What if you actually did marry him? You'd be his *third* wife behind Aspen Bauer and Tilly. And you'd be a stepmother to a baby named Cantaloupe. How could you possibly sign up for that?"

Emma just sat there, swirling her wine, considering the scenario. "Maybe I'm better off with Garrison."

"You should dump that old bastard. Just play checkers with him at the home once a week."

"You are so bad," Emma scolded.

"Speaking of bad, I have the most deliciously awful idea for a skit on *Laugh Track*." She paused a moment, wide-eyed. "Can we talk about something besides Dean Paul for a minute?"

Emma gave her a look. "Okay, but just for one minute."

Delilah's eyes brightened. "I'm thinking about a spoof of Mio and Mako, those stupid Japanese twins. Of course, that's probably oxymoronic. They basically spoof themselves. But still." She shrugged. "Could be wicked fun."

"I agree," Emma said, smiling broadly. "But we never had this conversation."

"Why?"

"I just got word that they're going to be de facto regulars on *The Beehive*."

Delilah's mouth dropped open in shock. "You're kidding."

Emma splayed out her hands in a gesture of dismay. "The audience loves them. They test very high."

"What's happened to America?" Delilah wondered. "We make stars out of Flavor Flav and Nicole Richie and now the Kometani girls. If Elizabeth Taylor were starting over today, she wouldn't have a fucking chance in hell of making it."

Emma thought about the comedy potential of skewering Mio and Mako. "How could you make them more ridiculous than they actually are?"

"I'll write a bit where they make out with each other. That'll guarantee attention in the writers' room and probably airtime, too."

"So you're just distracting them with a lesbian sister fantasy."

"I've learned the hard way that writing the funniest skit isn't good enough. The old guard feminists must be proud.

They blazed all those trails, and now we live in a culture where women take off their tops for a *Girls Gone Wild* hat and consider themselves empowered because of it."

Emma laughed. "Yeah, but if we were in college right now, that would totally be us."

"Oh, I have no doubt," Delilah agreed, pushing her half-eaten meal to the side. "Being a slut is so acceptable now, and I'm sure that I'd fall right in line." She studied Emma for a moment. "So are you going to be able to stand it if Dean Paul and Tilly get divorced? I mean, are you going to be, like, 'Oh, my God! He's available!'"

"I thought we weren't going to talk about him tonight."

Delilah looked exasperated. "We have to talk about guys. That's what we do. And I don't want to talk about the fact that you're sleeping with your grandfather. That's just gross. So until you meet someone else, Dean Paul it is."

Emma reflected on the possibility. "I don't see him going from a separation or a divorce to making a commitment to me."

"Maybe you're not such an idiot after all," Delilah said.

The wine was getting to Emma. She could feel the melancholy building. "I'm not delusional," she began with philosophical directness. "Deep down, I know that the circumstances will never be there to match the feelings I have . . . but that doesn't change my feelings, you know? They are what they are. All I know is that it hurts, and it's lonely, and sometimes I feel like I'll never, ever get over him." She sighed deeply and looked at Delilah, waiting for the verbal ax to swing.

But her friend just stared at her with uncharacteristic sweetness and concern, as if she wanted nothing more than to take this pain away. "Maybe you should think about seeing a therapist."

"Do I sound crazy?"

"No, but you sound like someone in a difficult situation,

and a good therapist could help you sort things out. I go periodically for emotional tune-ups."

Emma was stunned. "Seriously?"

Delilah nodded. "Just think about it. Listening to the voice in your own head all the time isn't the healthiest way to live." She paused to take a sip of wine. "And you damn sure don't follow my advice. I say it's time for reinforcements."

Emma nodded vaguely. "Maybe." She checked her watch and gasped. "Shit, I can't believe it's this late. Garrison had a meeting, but he's probably been waiting on me for two hours."

Delilah opened her mouth to speak.

Emma raised a halting hand. "I know you don't like him, but—"

"You're right," Delilah cut in. "I don't like him. But more importantly, *you* don't like him, either."

"That's not true—"

Delilah shook her head. "Emma, you never talk about Garrison. It's always Dean Paul, Dean Paul, Dean Paul. So please—just end it. If for no one else, do it for him. I mean, even that old bastard deserves someone who actually gives a shit."

Emma sat there as the rattling words killed whatever buzz the wine had generated. "You're right," she said quietly. "You're absolutely right."

"And I have been since you accepted the second dinner invitation from him. But who's keeping track?"

They split the tab and stepped out onto Eleventh Street. Emma breathed in the cool New York air and decided to end things with Garrison that night. Her BlackBerry vibrated. She swiped it from her purse just as the ring tone commenced. "Hello?"

"This is just a courtesy call." It was Tilly Lockhart. "You can have him. He's all yours."

Emma's insides rioted with a storm of emotion. For long seconds, she said nothing.

"I just wanted you to know," Tilly went on acidly. "Again, as a courtesy."

"I should hang up now, because if courtesy to other women is really your goal, then you'll be working the phone all night." Emma disconnected the call.

Delilah gazed at her expectantly.

"That was Tilly. Calling out of *courtesy* to tell me I could have Dean Paul." Her mind was still reeling—from the news . . . with the possibilities. "I guess she left him."

"If I saw my husband dancing like that with Juicy, I'd leave him, too," Delilah said.

Emma stood by the curb, passively awaiting a cab, not quite ready to leave. So, of course, a taxi jerked to a stop right away, triggering instant pressure to get inside.

"This isn't a hopeful development," Delilah said meaningfully. "Keep telling yourself that."

Emma nodded and slipped into the rear cabin. The ride home was a blur. She remembered calling out her address to the driver, then gazing out the grimy window. All of a sudden, she was standing in front of her apartment building.

With an aching sense of dread, Emma glanced upward. She knew Garrison was there . . . waiting for her. He wanted to have sex. He wanted to talk business. He wanted to gripe about politics.

But Emma simply wanted to be alone. She considered checking into a hotel. Garrison was strange in that he owned incredible properties throughout the city but preferred the cozy environment of Emma's small one-bedroom unit.

She hesitated, then ventured upstairs, determined to say what needed to be said, what should have been said a long time ago. The moment she turned the key in the lock, his voice rang out.

"Babe?" Garrison shouted from the bedroom. "I was starting to get worried."

"I had dinner in the Village with Delilah," Emma called back, frozen in the doorway. She was there, in that moment of chilling realization when something was so over that the word over did not do it justice.

"Bring me a fresh drink," Garrison said.

Emma cringed. She knew there would be a scene. He would be angry and hurt and demand to know why. She did not want to explain. She just wanted him to leave.

Steeling herself with a deep breath, Emma approached the doorway of the bedroom and stood quietly.

Garrison was naked and sitting up in bed. With his thick reading glasses perched on the end of his bulbous nose, he studied *The Wall Street Journal* while the television blared CNN and Anderson Cooper. For a long moment, he did not notice her. When he did, he gave her an odd look. "Where's my drink?"

"This isn't working, Garrison." The words came out before Emma had a chance to edit them in her mind.

He shrugged and turned his attention back to the newspaper. "That's usually my speech, but I'm a big boy. I can take it." And then he continued reading.

Emma watched him, stupefied. Not only was there no hurt or anger to speak of, there was not even the slightest hint of interest as to why she wanted to break up. "That's it?"

Garrison did not look up. "If it's not working for you, it's not working for you. I get it." He read for a moment longer. "How about that drink?"

Emma was simultaneously dismayed and infuriated. "Do you actually plan on sleeping here tonight?"

He tossed her a glance. "No good-bye fuck?"

Emma glared at him. "I'm taking a shower. Be gone by

the time I get out." She made a beeline for the bathroom and shut the door. Then she turned on the water full blast to muffle the sounds of her tearful breakdown.

Garrison behaved like it was nothing, like she was nothing. In a strange way, it was reminiscent of the way Dean Paul had treated her, too. Her crying jag intensified.

Maybe she was nothing.

THE IT PARADE
BY JINX WIATT

Fill in the Blanks

It used to be so easy for the caddish man who got the heave-ho. He'd either play house with the woman (usually a slut) who got him kicked out in the first place, or he'd crash on the couch of a buddy (usually a creep that the girlfriend/wife hated) who waxed lyrical on the glories of single guydom. America's jilted prince (his heiress wife said goodbye and amen) chose a more complicated situation with door number three: Bunking with the gay friend who openly swoons over him. Only in the new millennium, darlings.

19
Finn

"Tilly kicked me out," Dean Paul said, his voice casual and lacking any emotion. He could have just as easily announced, "Tilly gave me a sweater for my birthday."

Finn hung on the line, suddenly seized by an intense anxiety. What upended him the most was the immediate sense of the unknown.

They had a routine—Finn and Dean Paul—built around Dean Paul's *Hollywood Live* gig and his marriage to Tilly. When they talked, when they worked out, when they grabbed lunch— it was all dictated by Dean Paul, and Finn always made himself available to take advantage of his company.

Finn's reaction to this announcement that the inevitably doomed marriage had become an imminently doomed one was fear. After all, their friendship had been sealed in the crucible of Tilly's insistence that Dean Paul relinquish his ties to his carousing straight buddies. With Tilly out of the picture and Dean Paul's notorious history of forming attachments and then moving on with little remorse, the possibility for the whole connection to evaporate was there.

This scenario swirled inside Finn's mind as he hesitated,

searching for the right words. Finally, he spoke. "Are you okay? Do you want to meet for a drink and talk about it?"

"Yeah, that sounds good," Dean Paul said. But his tone was mocking. "Will you hold my hand and encourage me to *feel the pain*?"

Finn felt stupid. And Dean Paul had an uncanny knack for making him feel that way. "Your wife just dumped you. I thought you might be upset. For a minute there I forgot about what an incredible asshole you are."

Dean Paul laughed. "I need a place to crash for a couple of days. Do you mind?"

Finn's heartbeat picked up speed. "You want to stay with me?"

"If it's inconvenient, I can just go to a hotel."

"No!" Finn exclaimed, his protest coming out far more desperate than he intended.

"Okay, calm down, I'll stay with you. Jesus."

"No . . . I mean . . . it's no inconvenience. Really."

"Good. Because I'm right outside your building."

Finn rushed to the window and gazed down.

There, sixteen floors below, standing on the sidewalk with an overnight bag in his hand, was Dean Paul Lockhart.

Finn experienced a moment of pure rapture, though he felt positively imbecilic as a result. He was a well-educated man who had traveled all over the world. That this could be the most fantastic thing he had ever seen in his lifetime just seemed pathetic. But it truly was.

"Can you handle it?" Dean Paul asked.

As he watched him from above, Finn touched the window-pane, downright giddy over the fact that Dean Paul had come to him in crisis. "Handle what?"

"Me sleeping in the next room."

"I'll try to manage."

"Just in case you can't control yourself, I'm sleeping with a Taser gun."

"Hey, that sounds like kinky fun. Come on up." Finn disconnected the call, then tidied up the apartment in a mad frenzy until the fateful sound of three loud knocks rapped the door.

Finn sucked in a deep breath and stepped over to open it. "Just so you know—you're not the first unhappily married man to show up here unannounced."

Dean Paul smiled. "Oh, I have no doubt." He walked inside, surveying the sixties mod décor with an affirmative nod. "Nice place."

"Thanks."

"I can't believe I've never been up here."

"Well, consider it home."

Dean Paul gave him a strange look.

"For as long as you want to stay," Finn clarified.

"That's sweet. Does a robe come with that? Maybe a pair of slippers?"

"Okay, dickhead, I give up. The study's all yours. You'll have to move the desk to fold out the sofa bed. Sheets and blankets are in the hall closet."

Dean Paul stepped toward the bedroom and peeked inside. "Is that a queen size bed?"

Finn gave him a fuck you smile. "What else?"

"It looks comfortable. What's the problem? You can't share a bed with me and keep your hands to yourself at the same time?"

Finn regarded Dean Paul carefully, stunned to discover that he appeared to be serious. "You want to sleep in the same bed?"

"I don't *want* to, necessarily, but it sure beats a lumpy sofa bed."

Finn fought to contain his excitement and delight over the idea. In a faux display of no-big-deal, he shrugged. "It's fine with me." One beat. "Unless you snore, of course."

Dean Paul shook his head. "You won't even know I'm there."

Hardly. Finn knew that the proximity alone would keep him up all night. "Okay."

Dean Paul broke out into a gotcha smile. His teeth gleamed. "Dude, I'm not going to sleep with you."

Finn fought a superhuman battle not to let his disappointment show.

"The sofa's fine," Dean Paul went on. "I'll already be making one of your dreams come true by staying over. Two would just be spoiling you rotten." He laughed at his own joke. "I need to get hammered. What do you have to drink?"

"Vodka." He glanced over at the near-empty bar. "And more vodka."

"That'll get the job done," Dean Paul said. He dropped his bag with a thud and kicked back on the living room couch with a frustrated sigh. "This won't be a clean break like the last time. I said good-bye to Aspen and never had to look back. But I've got a kid with Tilly. I'm always going to be linked to that crazy bitch."

Finn busied himself prepping a batch of dirty martinis. "Were you asking for it?"

"Asking for what?"

"For her to tell you to leave." He dashed into the kitchen for ice and proceeded to shake up the night's poison, not bothering to talk over the ear-piercing rattle. When he finished, he went on. "The scene at the club with that girl . . . well, let's just say it was anything but discreet."

"Nothing happened. I barely dry-humped her."

"And if Tilly hadn't shown up . . . would it have ended

there?" He poured, garnished each drink with a plump green olive, and headed over to the couch.

"Whose side are you on?" Dean Paul asked. He impatiently took possession of the martini and started to drink fast. "By the way, don't sit down yet. You might as well make me another one before you get settled."

"I'm on the side of logic," Finn said as he doubled back to the bar. He returned with a half-full bottle of Pravda and a shot glass. "There. My bartending skills would be wasted on you tonight anyway."

"So you think I asked for it? Where's your sense of male solidarity? Wait a minute. Don't answer that."

Finn glanced at the coffee table and zeroed in on Benji's sleek mobile phone, the one with the damning video of Dean Paul dirty dancing with Juicy, the one he had confiscated in exchange for the promise to help reintroduce Benji to the New York social scene and media influentials as something more than an opportunistic fraud. He reached for the device and played the little movie.

"How many times have you rubbed one out to that?" Dean Paul asked.

"You stupid fucker!" Finn roared. "If I hadn't stepped in, that shit would be all over YouTube and TMZ and every trashy entertainment show!"

Dean Paul laughed. "Play it again."

Finn rolled his eyes and did the honors.

"Man, I look pretty out of it," Dean Paul commented, watching himself with a smug sense of marvel. "She's hot, though. I should've fucked her." He finished the martini, ate the olive, and poured a generous shot of vodka. "I mean, same end result and everything. You know?"

Finn slammed the phone shut and tossed it back onto the coffee table.

"Who is she anyway?"

"As I understand it, her name's Juicy."

"And I bet she is. Get her number for me. I won't let you watch, but I'll give you a detailed play-by-play."

"So I'm already your hotel and your bartender, and now you expect me to be your pimp," Finn said. The sick part was that he was already factoring out in his mind how to track down Juicy.

"I know you want to be everything in the world to me, dude. I'm just giving you a chance. Take advantage of it while you can."

Finn tried to give Dean Paul a serious stare. But sometimes it was difficult to gaze too long. He was not merely good-looking or even exceptionally handsome. The man was beautiful. And with his naturally tousled hair, three-day beard growth, wrinkled white Oxford, and lived-in jeans, he was putting forth zero effort to be that way. Which made him even more gorgeous.

There was the rare benefit of no distractions tonight. Finn decided to take advantage of *that*. "Why do you say those things?" he asked.

"What things?"

"You're always putting it out there that I'm obsessed with you and just praying for the day."

He gave Finn an annoyed look. "It's called a joke. I thought you could take one. My mistake."

"But it's a joke that never seems to end," Finn continued. "Sometimes it's funny. I mean, I can get a laugh out of it, too. But . . . sometimes I get the sense that you think of *me* as the joke. Like I'm just a stupid faggot."

"What are you talking about?" There was a wounded expression in Dean Paul's piercing blue eyes. "I never think of you that way. You're my best . . . you're a friend."

Finn's feelings were all over the place. He loved Dean Paul deeply . . . as a friend . . . and as someone more than that. The unrequited aspect was something that would probably never die. But hearing Dean Paul almost slip and utter the qualifier *best* in front of friend filled Finn with an almost nurturing sense of joy and pride.

"Don't pay attention to most of the shit I say," Dean Paul went on. "Sometimes I talk just to fill the airspace." He tossed back the first shot and poured another one. "I didn't realize it bothered you that much."

"Usually, it doesn't."

"I see the way you look at me sometimes, and it's not the way that a buddy looks at another buddy. Joking about it helps me deal. Takes the edge off, I guess."

Finn could feel his face grow hot. His cheeks were burning with embarrassment.

"I joke about it, but I'm not making fun of you. Well, I am, I guess. But not in a mean way. Does that make any sense?"

"You're being sensitively insensitive," Finn said.

"Yeah . . . *sensitively insensitive* . . . that's me. I talk smack to you, but I don't feel any attraction at all. I've never even been curious."

Finn had drained most of the martini and in spite of the awkwardness could feel himself start to relax.

Dean Paul laughed. "I can't believe this shit."

"What?"

"My wife kicks me out, and we're sitting here tiptoeing around your schoolgirl crush."

"Actually, you've made more references to that tonight than you have to Tilly, so I figured . . ."

"That I'd come rushing into your arms?"

Finn gave him a weary look. "Okay, let's talk about Tilly."

Dean Paul waved off the notion as he poured a third shot.

"Fuck that. I'm over it." He chased down the vodka. "Everybody's giving me a chance to start over."

"What do you mean by everybody?"

"Tilly dumped me. *Hollywood Live* fired me. I'm a free agent all the way around."

Finn lurched forward in alarm. "When did that happen?"

"This morning," Dean Paul said easily. "Today was a one-two punch." He seemed to be considering a fourth shot but made no move for it. "The show's tanking fast. It's probably a good thing not to be around when it officially dies."

"Yeah," Finn agreed absently, his mind taking in the sweeping impact of these changes. With no wife, no home of his own, and no job, Dean Paul had no reason to stay in New York. Granted, there was baby Cantaloupe. But Finn could easily see Dean Paul convincing himself that a long-distance parenting situation could work.

"Have you spent much time in Miami?" Dean Paul asked.

"Some," Finn answered, a sense of doom coming over him.

"I'm done with this city," Dean Paul said. "I'm moving to Miami."

THE IT PARADE
BY JINX WIATT

Fill in the Blanks

Having friends with money doesn't mean you won't find yourself flat broke. Just ask the gorgeous Black American Princess who's cohosting that new buzz-building TV chat hour. Her gal pal is an old money heiress with a modeling gig that pays point money. Her new beau is an entertainment mogul with a fleet of cars to his name, not to mention his own private jet. Meanwhile, the cash-strapped girl in question has been reduced to returning merchandise to snooty boutiques to pay off her sky-high bills. It's not necessarily the company you keep, darlings.

20

Simone

"I felt like a single mother before, so I hardly think this will be a radical adjustment," Tilly was saying. "And I plan on petitioning for full custody, of course. Dean Paul couldn't care for a Chia Pet properly. I've done everything as it relates to Cantaloupe's care."

"Where is she now?" Simone asked.

"With the nanny," Tilly said. "The one that *I* interviewed and hired. I'm telling you, I do *everything*. He packed an overnight bag when he left, and he's almost completely moved out. There are some clothes left but not much else. The furnishings in our apartment are things I picked out with the decorator. Again, he barely sat in on a single meeting. He was never truly invested in the marriage. All the signs were there, but I just chose to ignore them." She sighed deeply. "Okay, I've gone on and on about me. What's going on with you?"

"I've been so stressed lately," Simone began. "I got overextended on my—"

"Did I tell you that I called your fellow cohost?" Tilly cut in. "Emily."

"Emma," Simone corrected.

"Whatever," Tilly huffed. "Anyway, I called her right up and told her she could have Dean Paul. And then later that very same night she broke up with that geriatric magazine publisher she was dating." Tilly shook her head. "So pathetic. If they get together, I give it a month." She glanced at her near empty wineglass and rudely snapped her fingers to a passing waitress. "Do I have to fly to the Napa Valley and stomp grapes, or can you fix this problem?" She tapped the rim of her glass with a manicured nail.

The waitress was momentarily taken aback. "I'll see about it right away. What were you drinking?"

"I thought that was your job to know things like that," Tilly snapped. "You'll have to ask our runaway waiter. I haven't seen him in ages. He's probably in the bathroom getting stoned."

Simone was appalled. In a meager attempt to overcompensate, she gave the waitress a reassuring look.

Tilly cast an annoyed glance around the restaurant. "The service used to be so much better here."

Simone said nothing. They were at Pastis in the Meatpacking District, and the service was—as always—impeccable.

The waitress swooped back with more red wine.

"Now that wasn't so difficult, was it, dear?" Tilly murmured. She beamed a direct look at Simone. "You were saying something?"

"Yes," Simone launched in again. "I got overextended on—"

"Wait—I almost forgot," Tilly interrupted. "This breakup with Dean Paul is happening *just* in the nick of time. Seriously. I feel like Kiefer Sutherland in an episode of *24*. He just got the ax from *Hollywood Live*. Is there anything worse than an unemployed husband and father? Can you imagine being married to that? It'd be like living in a black neighborhood."

Simone tensed up immediately. "*Excuse me?*"

"Oh, Simone, please," Tilly said dismissively. "Everybody knows that most black women are forced to raise their children alone because the fathers are either in jail or playing basketball in the park during what should be productive work hours. There was a study. I heard about it on talk radio."

Simone was surprised by her own reaction. Though never one to fall in line behind Al Sharpton and march in protest against injustices to black people, she was still insulted by Tilly's diatribe. She raised a halting hand. "I'm offended."

"Oh, me, too," Tilly went on, completely oblivious. "And you don't even have a baby. Yesterday, I saw a black woman struggling with her stroller and trying to get it down the steps of a subway entrance. No father in sight to lend a hand. In a way I could relate. Basically, I'm in the same position now. Maybe that makes me an honorary *sista* or something." She laughed a little and drank more wine. "I should do a seminar for them at The Learning Annex. You know, give the black girls some tips on being strong and raising a child alone. Take last night. I had this adorable interactive playpen delivered for Cantaloupe. Of course, it required assembly. I'm worthless. Nanny Veronika is more so. The Honduran housekeeper can barely speak a word of English, much less read it. And there are no instructions translated into Spanish. Only French and Japanese. Go figure. So I'm about to have a nervous breakdown, and then I remember reading about that Rent-A-Guy service in the Style section of the *Times*. I call, they send a very handy college boy over, he puts the playpen together within minutes, I write him a check for seventy-five dollars, and the crisis is solved."

"I might be going out on a limb here," Simone began dryly, "but I don't think unwed black mothers should be your target audience for this seminar."

Tilly paused in thoughtful consideration. "You're probably right. They'd never be able to afford Rent-A-Guy. And why torture them with talk of a service beyond their means? It'd be like showing them my jewelry. An exercise in cruelty to say the least."

"The very least," Simone grumbled.

"Oh!" Tilly exclaimed. "You got me off track. I was *trying* to tell you about the timing of giving up on Dean Paul." She leaned in conspiratorially. "I suspect that he might have peaked. Now to be fair, he still looks good. Scrumptious, in fact. He's in phenomenal shape and will age like a dream— the bastard. But he's just meandering, you know? He has no real purpose. And he's at the point in life where suddenly that quality is very unattractive, almost pathetic. I'm not sure women even find him that appealing anymore. And I'm speaking of women with high standards like myself. There will always be bar trash who want their way with him and romantic obsessives like Emily."

"*Emma.*"

Tilly rolled her eyes. "*Whatever.* But I think his Lothario ways have just grown tiresome. Even the columnists are done. They're so bored with him that they've reduced the gossip to floating around these gay rumors about Dean Paul and Finn. And for what? To create a modicum of excitement? I'm just thankful for the ironclad pre-nup. What's mine is mine. What's his is his. And the apartment deed is in *my* name, thank God. My parents gave it to *me* as a wedding gift. It should be a clean break. Except for Cantaloupe. But I'll fight him to the death on that issue. I've already retained all the A-list family lawyers in the city, so he'll have to go second-tier for representation. I'm not worried about it, though. He's a perpetual adolescent. Any judge will see that. I kicked him out of the apartment, and instead of checking into a hotel like an adult, he goes over to Finn's apartment to sleep on the couch. I mean, really, how frat boy."

"But is he a good father?" Simone asked.

Tilly reflected on the question. "Cantaloupe *does* adore him. Her face lights up whenever he's around. And I suppose he could be described as affectionate and attentive toward her."

"So why do battle on the issue of custody?" Simone argued. "*You* may be divorcing him, but your daughter isn't."

Tilly's lips tightened into a firm line. "It's very complicated, Simone."

"It sounds pretty simple to me. Put Cantaloupe's best interest ahead of your ego . . . if that's possible."

Tilly glared at her. "Exactly what frame of reference do you have? As far as I can see, the only living thing you're responsible for besides yourself is a stupid cat."

"Which I don't have a twenty-four-hour sitter for," Simone shot back.

Tilly shook her head, as if dismissing Simone altogether. "Honestly, I should be discussing this issue with someone who actually has a child. Now you were saying something about being stressed out and overextended? Let's move on to that, shall we?"

Simone just looked at her.

"And if this is a lead-in to you asking me for money, then stop before you start. It's my personal policy *not* to loan money to friends. Mixing the two can get very messy. And I can't be swayed, either, no matter what the circumstances are."

"I don't *need* a loan. It's true that I'm a bit strapped for cash at the moment, but my agent found me some lucrative opportunities that work around my schedule for *The Beehive*."

Tilly exchanged waves across the bistro with a junior socialite type. "We're on the host committee for a Pompe disease fund-raiser, and she was a no-show for the sponsors party. So tacky. She's just in it for the social angle. Doesn't care a thing about the cause."

"What is Pompe disease?" Simone asked.

"Some kind of gene mutation. I'm not really sure. It's very serious, though. Fatal in most cases. You should make a donation." Tilly cast a vicious glance as the waiter flitted past. "How long does it take to make a fucking salad? I'm starving." She sipped more wine. "I'm going to be drunk, too, if I don't get some food in my system. What were we talking about? Oh, your new *opportunities*. Please tell me you're not still signed with that awful Sue woman with the ugly last name. She's wretched. All she does is push soap actors for mall appearances and stupid ribbon cuttings. You could do much better. Especially now with the show getting so much attention."

Simone said nothing.

"Are you still with her?" Tilly asked, her face a mask of horror. "God, you poor thing. I'd give you a referral to my agency, but I don't believe in those kind of favors. Nobody paved the way for me to sign with my agent. I earned his interest on my own accord. So what kind of project has superagent *Sue* found for you?"

"It's for Target. I'm still waiting on the details."

"For your sake I hope it's a commercial and not a store opening. Can you imagine? All those people lining up for an autograph and first day bargains? Dreadful."

"As long as they're paying my fee, I don't care. Anyway, the important thing is this—I would *never* ask *you* for money," Simone said acidly. "No matter what the circumstances were."

"Good," Tilly replied crisply. "That means we respect each other."

Simone fought the urge to scream as she wondered why the two of them even bothered to go through the motions anymore.

The waiter returned with their lunches—a grilled vegetable salad for Tilly and the seared salmon with lentils and shitake mushrooms for Simone. Now at least they could concentrate on something besides the impossible task of trying to communicate with each other.

"So did you ever have dinner with Kevon Edmonds?"

The mention of his name brought an unexpected—and involuntary—smile to Simone's face.

"I'll take that as a yes," Tilly trilled. "Do tell."

"He's not what I expected at all. Very rough around the edges, which I typically don't like. I've always preferred more sophisticated men."

Tilly gave her a puzzled look. "I'd hardly call Tommy Robb *sophisticated*. Didn't he go straight from high school into the pros?"

Simone bypassed the question. "As I was saying . . . Kevon has that street edge, but he also has a very sweet, protective quality about him. And his success is undeniable. It's almost awe-inspiring the way he came from nothing to where he is today. I don't know. I find him intriguing." She moved the mushrooms around with her fork. "But . . ."

"There's always a but," Tilly said, her tone all knowing. "Put it on the table. I'll let you know whether or not it's a deal breaker. I'm good at this."

Simone wavered for a moment. "I'm not interested in being part of a harem or filling the *classy* girl slot in his lineup of women. And that's sort of the sense that I get. Another woman he sees confronted me outside the studio. At one point, I thought she was going to assault me." The revolting image of Luscious Brown flashed in Simone's mind. "Ugh. This woman was vile. She looked like a street hooker from Central Casting, and every other word out of her mouth was bitch and ho. I still can't reconcile the fact that we're interested in the same guy."

"So you really like him," Tilly observed, a note of surprise in her voice as she stabbed at a piece of eggplant.

"I'm interested," Simone clarified, still not ready to admit it. "*Cautiously*."

Tilly shrugged. "Well, in dealing with a man like that . . . you'd have to be exceedingly tolerant if not outright blind on occasion. He traffics in low culture. With that comes all sorts of obscene temptations that no man can resist, especially a black man from a poor background."

Simone tensed up again. "Tilly, if I don't meet the qualifications to offer up opinion on the subject of children, then I say you're equally unqualified to talk about matters of race."

"Oh, please," Tilly replied, rolling her eyes. "I'm simply stating the obvious. Does he drive around in an ostentatious limousine?"

Simone hesitated, then nodded.

Tilly returned a smug smile. "I'm sure he loves nothing more than to have some woman perform obscene acts while they drive around. It's all so decadently predictable. He's probably a fixture at all the luxury brand boutiques. Am I right?"

Simone just sat there.

Tilly sighed. "This is textbook, Simone. Just know what you're getting involved with. Here's a man who'd probably laugh in the face of any woman who suggested a monogamous relationship. I'm sure he feels entitled to some sort of Hugh

Hefner-like lifestyle. I predict a short-lived and volatile affair. If you ask me, it's not worth it. Don't even bother."

A short time later, Simone was ensconced in a cab, muttering silent curses about all things Tilly Lockhart. What a rude, self-absorbed, self-righteous, opinionated, culturally insensitive bitch! And yet Simone had said yes to plans with her later in the week. Was it possible to truly hate the people you called your friends?

The taxi jerked to a stop in front of the Christian Dior boutique. Simone paid the fare and swung out. Standing just outside the store, she hesitated, giving the shopping bag in her hand a shameful glance. It was killing her to return merchandise, especially this gorgeous hobo bag, but there was simply no other way to cover the American Express bill. Sacrifices had to be made.

Simone stepped inside and prayed that her friend Punch was working. It would make the transaction much easier and more pleasant. Maybe even fun. Punch would totally get the concept of blowing too much money on fashion. Together they might even get a riotous laugh out of the situation.

Shit. Punch was nowhere in sight. But her bitchy counterpart, Alexandra, was already staring Simone down, casting disapproving eyes on the Dior shopping bag in her left hand.

She approached with radioactive attitude. "May I help you with something?"

Simone cleared her throat. "Yes, I have a return."

"Was there a problem with the bag?" Alexandra asked. The implicit message in her tone suggested that the real problem was with Simone.

"No, the bag is wonderful. It's just . . . not appropriate for me at this time."

"How unfortunate," Alexandra sniffed as she carefully inspected the merchandise and studied the sales voucher. "I can issue a store credit."

"That sounds lovely, but I'd prefer that the credit go to my card. Thank you." She presented her American Express Gold.

Alexandra made no move to accept it. "I'm sorry. No refunds after seven days. Store credit only."

"I don't understand," Simone said.

"Our return policy is clearly stated on your receipt," Alexandra said, pointing to the large bold print at the bottom.

A sense of doom overcame Simone. "Certainly you can make an exception in this case. I'm one of your best customers."

But the impervious look on Alexandra's face seemed to indicate otherwise. She passed the package back to Simone. "Store credit only."

"*Fine,*" Simone huffed. "I'll just sell it on eBay and make a tidy profit."

Alexandra glowered. "Come to think of it, you do look like the online garage sale type. Good luck with that."

Simone was livid. The nerve! "Do you know what the only difference is between you and a Wal-Mart checkout girl?"

Alexandra raised her eyebrows haughtily.

"A better wardrobe," Simone hissed. And then she walked out of the boutique, hobo bag still in hand. After all, a store credit would make no dent in the rubble of debt that was threatening to bury her alive. She needed cash.

Her mobile chimed with the sound of an incoming text message. Simone checked it and stopped cold on the sidewalk.

HEY, BROKE ASS BITCH. NEED A LOAN? COME
BY AND EARN IT THE OLD FASHION WAY.

Tommy Robb had sent it. Simone was certain. The igno-
rant misspelling of OLD-FASHIONED gave the dumb ass away.
With an enraged gaze, she swept the area in every direction.
There was no sign of the crazy bastard. But Simone knew
that he was watching her.

She just knew it.

THE IT PARADE
BY *JINX WIATT*

Fill in the Blanks

Ultimatums are tricky things, dar-lings. If you're going to make one, be prepared to deliver on it. Fifty is *not* the new thirty. But that's pre-cisely what a certain half-century-aged talk show host thought when she threw down the tired old gaunt-let, "Either she goes or I go!" Maybe this *seasoned* pro's fountain of youth elixir (the erotic dedications of a twentysomething bartender) is delud-ing her into thinking she's anything but a lucky piece of set furniture. This homeless man's (even poor guys can do better, so I've downgraded the phrase) Barbara Walters just might get pushed aside.

21
Sutton

"You son of a bitch!" Sutton roared. "How could you go behind my back and enlist that opportunistic whore to pillow talk with Garrison Friedberg about a project I knew nothing about? *I'm* the creative consultant for this show!"

Jay Lufkin's expression was more beleaguered than fearful. "Sutton, please calm down."

The condescension in his tone did not escape her. She cut a glance to the collection of vintage *Star Wars* figurines lined up like toy soldiers on his credenza. "Oh, I'm very calm, Jay," she said menacingly. "I haven't even started to smash your miniatures yet."

"You're blowing this way out of proportion. There's no conspiracy. I just asked Emma to speak with Garrison and determine if there was enough interest for an initial meeting." He splayed open his hands. "That's it."

Sutton found Jay's new confidence and cool authority to be extremely irritating. Give the little prick some success, and suddenly he thinks he's goddamn Gelman from *Regis and Kelly*. "No, that's not it. That's not it at all. I was deliberately left out of the loop. Emma came to you with this, didn't she?"

"Actually, it was my idea."

Sutton stared at Jay, and much to her annoyance, she believed him. "One that you didn't run by me."

Now it was Jay's turn to be annoyed. "Sutton, you can barely display a shred of civility toward Emma on the air. I assumed that your feelings toward Garrison were even more caustic. Or would you have relished the idea of going to him and asking for his help in a business venture?"

Sutton seethed silently. "It doesn't matter. The magalog idea sucks."

"If that were really the case, you wouldn't have stormed in here like this," Jay countered. It *is* a good idea. That's why you're pissed off." He sighed. "But none of this matters anymore. Emma and Garrison broke up before the meeting got scheduled. Now she's not interested in asking for one, and I don't see him eagerly entering into a situation with two ex-girlfriends in the mix."

Sutton downloaded the tidbit about the breakup. For Emma's benefit, she hoped Garrison was currently dating a twenty-year-old. "He's not the only magalog publisher in the world."

"But he's the best," Jay said.

"Cristal is arguably the best, too. But that doesn't mean I won't drink Pierre Jouet. Why should we dismiss a potentially good idea just because *Emma* got traded in for a newer model?"

"You're probably right."

"I'm right about a lot of things," Sutton said. Sensing an opening, she settled into the seat opposite his desk and crossed her legs. "As the creative consultant for *The Beehive*, I have some concerns about the direction of the show."

Jay regarded her curiously. "Okay."

"As you know, Jay, I'm a veteran in this business. I've been on-air with the best of them at ABC, CBS, NBC, CNN, and Fox News. If I know anything at all, it's chemistry, that special magic that comes from combining the right personalities with the right program vehicle." She took in a deep breath. "I just don't feel like we have the right chemistry . . . at least not with this current assortment of talent. It's so difficult to nail down. It's a very delicate balance."

"Yes, it is," Jay agreed, studying her closely. "Very delicate indeed."

"I'd like to see us . . . *experiment* with the arrangement. We could compile a short list of potential names and bring them in as guest hosts."

"With an eye toward hiring the best one permanently?" Jay asked.

Sutton nodded. "Exactly."

"So you see this as an addition to the group?"

Sutton hesitated. "Actually, I think four is an ideal number."

"Just cut to it, Sutton. Who's your target?"

"I don't have a *target*, Jay. But if I'm being honest, and I feel like I can be with you . . . Emma feels out of place in this format. I realize that she has natural appeal to a very attractive demographic, but there's a better puzzle piece out there for us. We just have to find it."

He shook his head. "Our research says otherwise."

"I'm the creative consultant, Jay."

"You're absolutely right," he replied tersely. "And you just consulted. Thank you for your input."

Sutton rose up defiantly. "I feel very strongly about this issue. It's not going to end here in the office of a neophyte. Maybe the success of this show is getting bigger than you can competently handle."

"Don't, Sutton." His tone seemed to convey more sympathy than anger.

"I won't be *handled*, Jay. I'm a pro. I've got clout. I was re-

porting on presidential elections when you were still jerking
off in the family bathroom."

"Believe me, Sutton, the handling you get right here is
preferable to the handling you'll get from the White Glove
executives." His voice was harsh.

Sutton sensed danger but decided to call his bluff. "I'll
find that out for myself." She started to leave.

"You're wasting your time, Sutton," Jay said. This time his
tone was ominous.

She stopped at the door, keeping her back to him.

"Emma isn't going anywhere. She's the star. And her research numbers back that up."

Sutton swallowed hard.

"Your open hostility made for fun gossip in the beginning, but now it's making viewers uncomfortable," Jay went
on. "They want to see a maternal figure on the set, someone
with some real warmth." There was a pregnant pause. "An
offer went out to Paula Deen yesterday."

Sutton whipped around. "That country cook?" Her voice
was but half its full compass. "They want to replace me with
her?"

Jay waved it off. "She wants too much money. They'll
never come to terms with her."

Sutton could hardly breathe.

"I'm only telling you this because you sound like a woman
who's ready to issue an ultimatum."

"Maybe I am."

"Then be prepared to live up to your end of it."

Sutton had never felt like a bigger fool. Here she was plotting, scheming, and threatening to pull rank in an effort to oust
Emma Ronson. Meanwhile, the Powers That Be thought so
little of her own contribution that even a calorie-busting

short-order cook with multiple chins was deemed a worthy replacement.

The humiliation was total. And as she stood here so close to losing this job, she realized how much she desperately wanted it. *The Beehive* was a big, splashy hit. Riding the wave could change her life professionally and financially. Deep down, she knew that it would succeed—with or without her.

Jay seemed to pick up on her moment of humility. "It's not too late, Sutton. You can turn this around."

"It sounds like they want a grandmother, Jay," Sutton said quietly. "I'm the woman with nothing in her refrigerator but a bottle of champagne and a jar of olives."

He grinned at her. "All they want is a maternal figure. Mothers can come at you in a variety of ways. Just don't be the one who eats her young."

Sutton cracked a smile. "I don't want to lose this." Her voice broke on the last bit. "There's no place else for me to go right now."

"You still have a place here," Jay said gently. "All you have to do is reclaim it."

"You mean keep the seat warm until you find the next Florence Henderson?"

"I wouldn't call what you've been doing keeping the seat warm. Your chair is a block of ice."

Sutton was silent.

"You don't have to compete, Sutton," Jay told her. "You don't have to wear shorter skirts and date younger men. You've got twenty years—if not more—on every other cohost."

Sutton winced.

"And that's not a bad thing. It's nothing to try to hide or to be ashamed of. Your cohosts need your wisdom and your experience and your maturity. Give it to them, and you'll be giving it to the audience." Jay made gestures to Sutton's hair and clothing. "You put on a good front, but you're not comfortable with any of this. And the viewers aren't comfortable, either. This is morning television. It's intimate. You have to be natural."

She practically worked up a sweat trying to remain impassive. It was a bitter pill to swallow. Emma was the goddamn star. Finn was the TV virgin. Simone was the critics' dartboard. But Sutton was the one getting a lecture on what to wear and how to act if she wanted to keep her fucking job.

"I need some time." She managed to say it without breaking down.

Jay nodded.

Sutton left him there to wonder just how much. She tore into her dressing room, grabbed her purse, alerted the car service that she was ready, and stalked out of the studio without a word to anyone else.

The ride home nearly killed her. It was nothing more than a masochistic internal replay of the worst meeting of her career.

They want to see a maternal figure on the set.

Someone with some real warmth.

An offer went out to Paula Deen yesterday.

Just don't be the one who eats her young.

The remaining hours of the day loomed ahead like a torture sentence. Suddenly, it dawned on her that Scooter had the day off. He was at her apartment now, probably still sleeping on the forty-thousand-dollar mattress he claimed as a second residence. Sutton shook her head, completely torn. He was a hot stud but a stone-cold loser.

Oh, God, she did not want to see him or fend off his lame

attempts at conversation. Sutton yearned to be alone. Suddenly, she reconsidered. Scooter might be good medicine for the pain after all. He could fuck her silly. And then she could take a handful of Ambien and zone out for the next forty-eight hours. Yes. That was a beautiful plan.

To avoid any engagement from the too-chatty doorman, she pretended to be talking on her cell phone as she swept through the lobby and into the elevator.

Sutton entered her apartment. From the bedroom, she could make out the low mumble of Scooter's voice. She walked back to greet him.

"Oh, it's a sweet setup, man." He was naked and flat on his back, staring at the bedroom ceiling as he talked on her cordless telephone and scratched his balls. "I'll lose a bet like this anytime. Just bring it on."

Sutton halted outside the door and continued to listen. She did not want to . . . but she could not stop herself.

"She's not that bad of a fuck, dude," Scooter went on. "I'm serious. The bitch never had a kid, so her cunt still has some grip. Shit, I've nailed women ten years younger than this who were in worse shape. One lady took off her panties, and her labia drooped down." He laughed. "I thought it was going to hit the floor, dude . . . I'm not joking . . . You know it . . . Hell, yeah, she's rich. She sleeps on a fucking mattress that cost forty grand . . . Yeah, I've racked up some pretty decent shit—an Xbox, clothes, shoes. And not crap from The Gap, either. Real designer shit . . . No doubt . . . I think I want her to pay off my credit cards next. I need that shit out of my life . . . No, I think she will . . . All I have to do is shove my cock in her mouth. She can't get enough of it." He laughed again. "I'll see you guys later tonight. Let's pick up some young hotties for a change. I've forgotten what a tight pussy feels like . . . Okay . . . Later." And then he hung up and drifted back to sleep.

For the longest time, Sutton stood there, statue still, wondering what to do. Finally, the answer came to her. Just steps away in the master bath medicine cabinet was the Ambien.

The whole bottle would get the job done.

THE IT PARADE
BY JINX WIATT

Fill in the Blanks

When it comes down to breakups, here's the golden rule: Always be the one to do the leaving. Not only does that make for a much better story (the girl who sobs over the guy who left her is about as much fun as lung cancer), but it ratchets up the quality of talent in the rebound pool. Why? A dejected girl is easy prey. The lady who presses the EJECT button is a true score. Too bad that young morning talk starlet can no longer claim to have marched out on that startlingly virile publishing magnate. Turns out Mr. Viagra was up to no good with two delicious tarts long before he was shown the exit door.

22

Emma

"It was so funny," Mio Kometani said breathlessly. "I thought Mako had cleaned up the poo poo, but she thought that I had! So it was still there the next morning." She held her nose. "Poo poo stinks." She giggled.

Mako giggled, too. "I didn't clean up the poo poo, but she thought that I had!"

Emma traded a brain-dead look with Finn.

"Now I've only seen a few clips of the show that feature your dog," Simone interjected. "But I understand that she's quite the diva."

"Oh, yes," Mio answered in a serious tone. "Her name is White Diamonds, and she's a Chihuahua from a champion bloodline."

Mako nodded. "She has a collar made of white diamonds, too."

"And one made of rubies and sapphires," Mio put in.

"She also has her own live-in chef," Mako said. "He only cooks for White Diamonds, and he's a graduate of the French Culinary Institute."

"Oh, well, *he* must've been at the top of his class," Finn cracked.

The audience roared with laughter.

Mio and Mako returned blank stares.

Emma glanced down at her notes for the segment, and for a fleeting moment, wondered if this could be the death knell for a career she had worked so hard to build. "Now what's this I hear about White Diamonds being psychic?"

"She is," Mio said earnestly. "She tells us what to wear and what songs to sing."

"And she tells us what clubs to go to," Mako added.

"Exactly how does White Diamonds do this?" Emma inquired, hating herself for asking the question.

"She runs around, she barks, and sometimes she pees," Mio said. "It depends."

The audience responded with amused titters.

"If that's the case, why do I bother with telephone psychics?" Finn cracked. "It sounds like I could save myself a fortune by adopting a mutt from the pound."

More laughter.

Mio and Mako giggled dimly.

"The two of you manage to stay in phenomenal shape, and I understand that a diet book is in the works," Simone said.

Mio nodded enthusiastically. "Whenever we have time we scribble down ideas for our diet book. Like when we go out to a restaurant for dinner, we always order three or four entrées. That way when the food comes, you know that you can't eat all of it, and you start to feel full right away."

"Yes," Mako chimed in. "I just take a bite from each dish, and then I'm stuffed!"

Emma just sat there, appalled. "How could the average person afford to do that? And what about the obscene waste of food?"

Mio and Mako looked stunned. Clearly, such concerns had never entered their cotton candy minds.

"I think it's time for a song!" Finn erupted, exaggerating

the awkward moment save for full comic impact. "What are you going to sing for us today?"

Mio cleared her throat. "Today we are singing a very special song called 'The Prayer.'"

Mako beamed proudly. "And we are dedicating it to all of the models with eating disorders."

Emma did an involuntary double take and nearly toppled over.

Finn steadied her with a firm hand. "I think Emma is already overcome with emotion."

"Yes," Emma managed to say through clenched teeth. "If only I could describe precisely what I'm feeling."

The treacly strains of canned karaoke music commenced as Mio and Mako teetered off set toward a small stage where two wireless microphones awaited them.

They began to sing the Andrea Bocelli and Celine Dion classic in breathless voices devoid of personality—and clearly aided by pre-recorded vocal overlays. "I pray you'll be our eyes/And watch us where we go . . ."

"This is for the runway models who won't eat," Emma muttered under her breath.

"Wounded war veterans and the crisis in Darfur were already taken," Finn murmured.

"I used to be a journalist," Emma whispered tragically to no one in particular.

"This *is* news," Finn whispered back. "It's an act of terrorism set to music."

Emma struggled to contain her laughter, then morphed into more serious mode when she caught the look of consternation being leveled against her by Jay Lufkin.

Thankfully, Simone had been blocked to appear with Mio and Mako at the close of the song and provide the lead-in for the next commercial break.

Somehow Emma managed to endure what remained of the show with some semblance of professionalism—the cooking segment, an interview with a indie film actress about her latest *edgy* project, the obligatory before/after fashion makeover featuring a member of the studio audience.

When it was over, she bolted from the set, seeking immediate solitude.

But she was intercepted by Jay. "Emma, what's going on? You spent most of the show looking like you had someplace else to be."

"Maybe I do."

Jay regarded her curiously, a question in his eyes.

Emma sighed heavily and slumped against the studio wall as a phalanx of people scurried this way and that. "I don't know, Jay. I was sitting there with the Kometani twins, and it just hit me. What am I doing here? Talking about a psychic dog? Pretending to be interested in a stupid makeover that you could find on any local morning show? I feel like my brain is rotting already. I'll be a vegetable before the first season is over."

Jay opened his mouth to speak.

Emma raised a hand to halt him. "Don't say anything about *research*. I don't care about that right now."

"I'll admit—today's show was more fluff than usual. The segment mix was slightly off, and Sutton was gone. But still . . . I think you're overreacting," Jay said.

Emma shook her head, not convinced. "I can't sit there and talk about which idiot was supposed to clean up White Diamonds' shit."

"Emma—"

"I feel like an imposter, Jay. I realize that daytime is soft, but this is . . . it's embarrassing."

"It's a hit," Jay argued.

"So is *Maury*. But I'd never do that, either." She sighed deeply, thinking of her agent, Adam Moss, wondering if he could extricate her from this horrible mistake. It had been an emotional decision to leave *Today in New York*. She had believed that shaking up her life and embarking upon a new career would liberate her from the melancholy over Dean Paul . . . yet it was still front and center, crowding out more important things. Oh, God, she resented him for that. Hated him, in fact. Was that possible? To *hate* the man you thought you loved?

"Don't bail on me," Jay said. He was almost pleading. "We can fix this."

Emma gave him a doubtful look.

"The perfect formula isn't there, Emma. I'll admit that. What's working, what's not quite working—it's still a work in progress. And you're right—the softer segments were overpowering today."

Emma could feel herself caving in. She liked Jay. She trusted him, too. But deep down she sensed that the format of the show would never lend itself to becoming the kind of program she needed to be a part of.

"There's an opportunity in the 'Bee in Our Bonnet' segment," Jay said eagerly. "You can talk about any issue of the day."

Emma's faint smile was uncertain. "Don't take this the wrong way. Finn and Simone are great at what they do, Jay, but I'm not sure engaging them in a discussion on the crisis in the Middle East is the best way to give *The Beehive* some gravitas."

Jay registered a look of panic. When he spoke, his voice was half its full compass. "Emma, you're the anchor to this enterprise. Your approval numbers exceed your cohosts two- to threefold. If you want changes, we can discuss them." He paused a beat. "Even big changes."

She really looked at Jay to determine his meaning. "As in *talent?*"

Jay nodded severely.

Emma was shocked to discover that her popularity rendered her such power. "That's not what I want, Jay—"

"I realize that the situation with Sutton has been strained at best. There's already—"

"I'm not asking you to fire Sutton Lancaster," Emma hissed. She glanced around to make certain that no one was within earshot. "This isn't an ultimatum. It's got nothing to do with her. Anyway, you told me that the research on her was solid."

"I said that it didn't *spike*," Jay corrected. "And I was being kind. I hoped that the negatives would level off. But it's not happening fast enough. This is just between us."

Emma nodded.

"She's not out the door yet, but an offer did go out to Paula Deen. Her interest is lukewarm, but if she accepts . . ."

Emma could hardly believe it. "*Paula Deen?* That Southern woman who cooks like we're still living in the fifties?"

Jay opened his mouth to answer.

But Emma thundered on. "Taking Sutton Lancaster out of the equation and putting Paula Deen in makes this situation even worse for me." She shook her head and started to walk away. "I can't do this, Jay. I'm sorry. This was a mistake." Her next words were impulsive ones. But for once the decision she made had nothing to do with Dean Paul Lockhart. In fact, he had scarcely entered her mind. A gut instinct told her that it was the right thing to do.

"I quit."

THE IT PARADE
BY JINX WIATT

Fill in the Blanks

New York's nightclub scene has definitely seen better days, darlings. Get a club impresario talking, and he/she will bore you to tears with complaints about party-stomping police (they hate noise and cigarettes) and weekend bridge-and-tunnel riffraff (they shop cheap boutiques and wear bad jewelry). So talk of a VVIP (the extra V is *not* a typo) establishment being dreamed up by America's popular new gay blade and a *very* surprising business partner has the tongues of boldface names wagging like crazy.

23

Finn

"Finn, please don't let on that it's me. If he's there, just say so, and I'll hang up."

"He's not here, Tilly. I'm not sure where he is. The gym, probably."

"Well, I have no doubt that you're taking Dean Paul's side in all of this, but I hope you can at least grant me a civil conversation."

"I'm not on anyone's side," Finn insisted wearily, insulted but not surprised by her assumption.

"Oh, of course not," Tilly trilled sarcastically.

Finn experienced a quick flash of anger. "Tilly, you called me. I answered. And I've given you no indication to think that Dean Paul has somehow turned me against you. Now, what do you want?"

"What do I *want*? Oh, that's charming. And you say there's no bias."

Briefly, Finn shut his eyes. Perhaps Tilly and Dean Paul deserved to be married to each other. "I know this is a difficult time for you, too," he said gently. "Is there anything I can do?" One beat. "Maybe you'd like to move into my apartment and not clean up after yourself."

"How funny. I just got rid of a roommate like that." Her tone carried a bitter edge. "Seriously, Finn, I need your honest, unbiased take on something. I'm having a childcare crisis."

"Is something wrong with the baby?"

"No, Cantaloupe is absolutely fine. But I'm without a nanny at the moment."

"What happened to—"

"Veronika? Oh, it's been dreadful. She spends half her life online looking for a sister that she claims is trapped in a prostitution ring somewhere in Germany. I thought that only happened to beauty pageant contestants in Saudi Arabia. Anyway, she gave me some ridiculous story about finding her in Amsterdam and had the audacity to ask me to pay for her to travel there and bring her sister back. Are you believing this? Naturally, I refused. I mean, I'm not running a travel agency for runaway prostitutes. But now some of my jewelry is missing. And—surprise, surprise—so is Veronika. She never showed up this morning, and I finally put it all together. Finn, I need you to be honest with me. What kind of state is Dean Paul in? Could he be trusted with Cantaloupe? I only ask this because I'm in a horrible bind. I'm due in L.A. for a 24/7 event that I can't possibly reschedule. It's a new product launch, and executives from all over the world are flying in. It's for an amazing eye cream that retails for five hundred dollars. But it's worth every penny. It's made from horse semen. I'll bring you back a free sample. Anyway, I can't possibly hire a new nanny, check references, and have a background report done in a day. I could take her with me, but she was running a fever a couple days ago, and I don't trust the cabin air on commercial flights— too many germs. So I'm at my wit's end and actually considering Dean Paul for the task of taking care of her until I get back. It's just an overnight trip. So has he been drinking heavily? Be honest. I know you adore Cantaloupe, so think of her welfare before you answer."

"I think it would be good for him to spend some special time like that with his daughter," Finn said. "And I say that without a moment's hesitation."

Tilly breathed a deep sigh of relief. "Thank you, Finn. I don't know why I needed to hear that. I've trusted a kleptomaniac Russian whore with my daughter for days on end, but I second guess the child's father and the man I married. Go figure. I'll call him. Hopefully, we'll be able to stop screaming at each other long enough to work out the small details."

"I hope it works out."

Tilly was uncharacteristically silent. "Me, too," she finally said.

"Try his cell," Finn suggested. "Wherever he is, I know that he's got it with him."

"Finn," Tilly began hesitantly. "Has he . . . has he talked about us?"

Now it was Finn's turn to hesitate. "Tilly, I can't be put in the middle like that. It's not fair. We've talked about a lot of things. I'm not taking sides here, but I have to honor his confidence. I owe him that allegiance."

"Of course," Tilly said quickly, obviously stung by the rebuke but recovering fast. "It was stupid of me to ask."

"Tilly—"

But before Finn could get another word out, she had already hung up.

He wavered between calling her back and letting it go, ultimately deciding on the latter. After all, the only way to spare Tilly's feelings would be to lie. It seemed cruel to pass along the news that Dean Paul was resigned to a divorce, that in his heart and mind he had moved on, that he was already plotting a relocation to Miami. Better to allow her to go on thinking that he might be quietly devastated.

Five rhythmic knocks rapped the door.

Finn checked the peephole to see the new and definitely not improved Benji Patt standing outside his door. With great annoyance, he flung it open. "You should call first."

Benji gave Finn a diffident shrug and brushed passed him to enter the apartment, smugly surveying the surroundings. "Everything looks pretty much the same."

"Well, I did have the place fumigated after you left," Finn said pointedly.

Benji appeared unfazed by the remark. His eyes zeroed in on Dean Paul's gym bag, which was carelessly slung on the living room floor, its contents sloppily spilling out. "Hmm . . . apparently, it didn't take."

"What do you want?" Finn demanded.

"A friendlier hello for starters."

"This is as good as it gets."

Benji spied his mobile phone on the coffee table and stepped over to retrieve it. "I never got around to signing up for new service. Do you mind?"

Finn gave him a ho-hum look of disapproval. "I don't care. It hardly ever rings. You must not be very popular. Anyway, the movie's been deleted."

Benji rolled his eyes. "Anything to protect your straight and married boyfriend, right? That relationship must be *so* fulfilling." He settled onto the couch. "Aren't you going to offer me a drink?"

"No. You've stayed too long already. Now, again, what do you want?"

"A plan," Benji announced. "You promised to reintroduce

me to the right people in New York, make some business connections." He looked up expectantly. "I'm ready."

"Yeah, well, I'm not. I'll call you. Maybe this weekend. There's a big thing at Stereo."

"I want to start my own blog," Benji announced. "Gossip items, pictures of me with celebs, that sort of thing."

"Just what the world needs."

"If that fat queen Perez Hilton can do it, why can't I? I figure all I need is a new laptop, a photographer to follow me around, and some decent connections."

Finn felt a moment's pure sympathy for the man currently known as Benji. His desperation for celebrity access seemed worse than ever. It was pathetic to see someone pushing to create a life that resembled nothing of his own. What a loser. And to think that Finn had once been in love with the guy. Frightening. Must have been the fierce looks. Finn had always been such a goner for beauty. That explained Benji then. It explained Dean Paul now. But Benji's presence was having no effect on him. The total lack of substance was countervailing his physical appeal. A sure sign of growth if ever there was one.

Finn gestured to the door. "Keep Saturday night open for now. I'll let you know about Stereo."

Benji made no move to leave. "I need to meet someone with deep pockets. How much does it cost to open a night-club?"

"More than you have and more than you can get."

Benji's eyes lit up. "I hear everyone complaining about the club scene. Bloomberg's pissing all over it. The tight asses with their neighborhood noise ordinances are shutting down hot spots. Trash from New Jersey buses in to perpetrate on the weekends. And is there really a quality joint for A-listers? You know, a place where Paris and Lindsay can't bring their juvenile shit?"

Finn just looked at Benji. "Un*fucking*believable!"

Benji stared back, his expression stunned and vacant.

This only intensified Finn's anger. "We've had this conversation before, asshole!" He pointed to the bedroom. "In that bed! Only it was me saying those words . . . practically verbatim! You might as well be lip-synching right now!"

"That was, like, a year ago," Benji argued lamely. "I can't remember who said what."

"You didn't say *anything*!" Finn roared. "It was *my* idea! I've dreamed about opening a club since my days at Brown! Have you ever had an original thought in your whole stupid life?"

Benji appeared bulletproof. "It's not like opening a club is the most original idea in the world. Do you own the patent on it?"

Finn tried to shake off the urge to punch Benji in the face. "You're giving me a headache. Please go."

"We could do it together."

Finn glared at him.

"As business partners," Benji clarified. "Nothing more."

"More like nothing at all," Finn hissed. "And what exactly would classify you as a business *partner*? You have no capital to invest, and you don't know shit about the club industry—except how to get kicked out of one after they wise up to your drink-and-dash routine."

There was the sound of a jangling key. And then Dean Paul walked through the door. He halted right away. "Sorry. I didn't realize you had company."

Finn waved off the concern. "He was just leaving."

Benji made no move to get up. "I don't have to." He gave

Dean Paul a hardcore, lascivious look. "I'm game for a three-way."

Finn grabbed Benji's forearm and roughly pulled him to his feet. "It's time for you to go. Seriously."

"Okay, okay," Benji whined, shaking free of Finn's grip. "You want him all to yourself." Another lewd stare at Dean Paul. "I can see why."

Dean Paul made eye contact with Finn.

"Trust me. Introductions are *not* necessary," Finn explained, red hot with embarrassment and pushing Benji toward the door.

"I'll keep Saturday night wide open," Benji shouted, more for Dean Paul's benefit than for Finn's. "Don't forget to call me!"

Finn slammed the door and double bolted the lock, then leaned against it with a deep sigh of relief. He glanced down at the floor, barely able to make eye contact. "Long story."

Dean Paul cracked a smile. "Next time we get hammered, you'll have to tell me all about it."

Finn loved it whenever Dean Paul spoke in the future tense. His trust in the relationship . . . the friendship . . . whatever it was . . . never managed to solidify. Part of him always feared that Dean Paul might end things automatically. And the recent talk of a Miami move only heightened that fear.

"Tilly called," Finn announced, anxious to bury the topic of Benji.

Dean Paul nodded. "That's why I'm back. Looks like I'm moving back in." One beat. "For a night or two at least. She's got this big modeling thing, and the nanny bailed." He shook his head, deep in thought. "It's crazy."

"Yeah, she told me."

"This will be the most time I've ever spent alone with my

daughter. I think it'll be cool." He stepped over to his gym bag and began to push the overflowing contents back inside. "Anyway, thanks for the crash pad. I've probably cramped your style long enough."

Finn's heart sank at the reality of Dean Paul leaving. Because having him here—sleeping on the couch, junking up the place with his dirty clothes and wet towels—was just like a fantasy . . . and probably the closest thing to the kind of relationship Finn dreamed about that would ever be realized.

"I found a realtor in Miami," Dean Paul announced casually. "She sounds like a go-getter. I'll probably head down there in a few days and look at some places."

The news killed Finn a little bit. His stomach was instantly in a million little knots . . . and his mind was instantly in hyper-drive, thinking of a way to keep Dean Paul in New York.

THE IT PARADE
BY JINX WIATT

Fill in the Blanks

If ever there was a sign that feminism might be a lost cause, then it is any young woman engaged in a relationship with a certain hip-hop mogul. This urban high roller fancies himself as a modern-day king of decadence. It's *his* world. And the women in his court are just living in it. Hopefully that too-lovely-for-words Black American Princess (she's a *buzz* beauty with some serious personal finance issues) will remember that Helen Reddy ("I Am Woman") came before Britney Spears ("I'm a Slave 4 U").

24
Simone

"This is too tight. Bring me the next size up."

"What do you have on now?" Simone asked.

"An eight."

Simone sifted through the Wal-Mart clothing racks. Apparently, ten was a popular size in Franklin, New Jersey. There were plenty of fours, sixes, eights, twelves, and fourteens, but no tens. "I can't find a ten!" Simone called back to the fitting room. "Let's try another style."

"But I like this one!" the woman yelled.

"Then lose some fucking weight," Simone muttered under her breath.

"What did you say?"

"I said . . . you'll just have to wait and see if more tens come in," Simone answered.

This was a career low point. Perhaps the very lowest. Schlepping to a Wal-Mart in New Jersey to play celebrity personal shopper for a lousy two thousand five hundred dollars.

"It's easy money, sweetheart," Sue Hotchner had assured her. "You're just helping people shop for an afternoon. It'll be fun. I bet it won't even feel like work. I've got another client who'd do this all day long if I let her."

The woman stepped out of the fitting room, a fleshy white leg jutting out of a barely wrapped polyester wrap dress. "Something must be wrong. I can usually wear an eight." She looked to be on the verge of tears. "How did I get so fat?"

"Some garments are cut differently," Simone said, trying to be kind. "It's probably a very small eight." She gave her a comforting smile.

"Either that or I'm really a nine—on the fast track to a ten." The woman shook her head. "This was a bad idea. I took vacation hours at work to be here, because I never have any time to shop for myself. I've got three kids and a husband who travels all the time for his job." She shrugged miserably. "I thought you could work some star magic and make me look pretty. It probably wasn't meant to happen here anyway, but a Wal-Mart dress is about the only thing I can afford." Self-consciously, she closed the gap in the dress and shuffled back through the flimsy curtain of the fitting room.

"Does this look too slutty?"

Simone turned to see the thirteen-year-old she had been assisting earlier. The girl stood there in a skirt so small that it looked as if she had been squeezed into a sock with the toes cut off. "*Too* slutty? Sweetheart, there are no varying degrees of appropriate sluttiness. Any and all should be avoided. But the short answer is yes. Too slutty."

The girl flounced away, disappointed, maybe, but also better educated.

An obese woman stepped into Simone's personal space zone. "I had my colors done by a professional colorist, and she said that I should only wear peaches and browns. What do you think?"

Simone took a reflexive step backward. "I think black is

naturally slimming. It's also a wardrobe basic that nobody should avoid." A gnawing feeling of guilt kept ricocheting in Simone's mind. "Excuse me for a moment." She returned to the wrap dress rack that she had rummaged through just minutes before with barely a glance. This time she carefully checked the tag on each garment, and she was delighted—after all—to find a size ten. She rushed over to the fitting room. "Look what I found! Try this one!"

The expression on the woman's face was pure hope and gratitude.

And so on it went for another two hours, after which Simone was exhausted and slumped into the backseat of a Lincoln Town Car being transported back to New York. In a way, the experience had humbled her. She had been complaining about the meager money she was set to earn from the appearance only to meet a woman whose shopping trip to Zanzibar was a twenty-dollar Wal-Mart dress. The realization provided some keen perspective.

But now, speeding back toward Manhattan, Simone was once again preoccupied with her own woes. Though grateful for the Target and Wal-Mart appearance money, it failed to add up to much after Sue chopped out her cut (twenty percent) and another twenty-five percent was tucked away for taxes. What remained hardly put a dent in Simone's money problems. They had grown that severe.

Her anxiety over her finances had triggered a sleeping disorder that prevented her from resting through the night. Even Tylenol PM could not knock her out, and usually she reacted to those over-the-counter treatments as if she had been given a heavy narcotic. And *The Beehive* rumors were hardly a reason to sleep peacefully. Gossip was swirling that major changes were imminent. What with Sutton having missed the last few shows and hushed talk about Emma quitting,

Simone had no idea what to think. Even with none of the whispers zeroing in on her, she felt no sense of job security. Critics still pointed her out as a disposable set piece, and everyone on set from Jay to the grips seemed to regard her with a certain degree of ambivalence.

So her bank account was a wreck, her career was shaky, her ex-boyfriend was stalking her, she had stumbled into the role of Girlfriend Number Whatever to Kevon Edmonds, and her most trusted confidante was Tilly Lockhart, who rarely listened to a word out of anyone's mouth that was not about her.

Simone's cellular jingled. And who else would it be but Tilly calling to discuss Tilly. Simone had already been held hostage as she droned on about the nanny crisis. At almost every point in the story, Simone kept waiting for even the faintest sign of sympathy for Veronika's predicament. But apparently having a kidnapped sister in a German prostitution ring guaranteed you nothing from Tilly Lockhart. "Hi, Tilly."

"Where are you?"

"In a car on my way back from New Jersey."

"Oh, how awful!" Tilly cried. "I'd ask why, but I've had enough distressing news for one day. Listen, I wanted to let you know that I spoke with Dean Paul, and I've agreed to let him take care of Cantaloupe while I'm away. I see no other recourse, and I think it will be a good exercise for him to act like a responsible parent for once. I wish I didn't have to go, but the 24/7 people are paying me buckets of money, and the travel is first class, so it's hardly a root canal. Anyway, we had a civilized discussion. I suppose he might make a decent ex-husband after all. Although he did try to defend his dance floor romp with that bleached sack of bar trash by saying I had lost interest in sex. Can you believe that?"

"Have you?" Simone asked, grateful for the moment to be tackling someone's problems other than her own.

"Have I what?"

"Lost interest in sex."

"Simone, I'm a smart woman with two homes, a career, and a young baby. Of course, I've lost interest in sex. Plus, I take Lexapro to keep the edge off, and that medication really messes with your ability to climax. It takes *forever*. Trust me. And frankly, I don't have forty-five minutes to lay there while Dean Paul works harder than an illegal immigrant day laborer to prove that he can make me come. I mean, honestly. Just forget it. I'd much rather have the sleep than the orgasm. Now why on earth are you coming back from *New Jersey?*"

Simone simply did not have the energy to think up a lie. "Sue booked me for an in-store appearance at Wal-Mart, because I need the money."

For several long seconds, Tilly was silent. Finally, she spoke. "Your agent is a hack, Simone. Dump her."

"Tilly, I—"

"I'm serious. She thinks too small. If you're going to drag yourself to New Jersey and stomp through a Wal-Mart, then at least be there to promote your own product. You should have your own line of cheap clothes or something." Tilly let out an exasperated sigh. "*Please*. Listen to what I'm saying. Sue could never make any of this happen. And you have to act now while *The Beehive* is hot. Every single one of those *Queer Eye* boys made out like bandits. And several of those *Trading Spaces* people did the same thing. Laurie Smith has her own line of fabric. And now she's designing lamps."

Simone just sat there waiting for the insult to drop.

"You know what? I'm going to break my personal policy and tell my agency about your situation. I can't stand by and

watch you wallow in the kind of low-rent promotional opportunities that are meant for reality show stars. I mean, we're
closely associated with each other, and this could be damag-
ing to *my* reputation as well. So I'm going to have a conversation with Michael about someone's career other than my
own."

"How selfless of you," Simone sniffed, simultaneously
touched, grateful, and irritated.

"Well, let me go. I have a million things to do to prepare
Dean Paul for the care of sweet Cantaloupe. Now as soon as
I hang up, I want you to call Sue and fire her. It'll be the best
career decision of your life! Call me soon."

Simone briefly considered making the call to Sue but
ultimately decided to wait. It would be just like Tilly to
never have the talk with Michael, and then where would
Simone be?

She faded in and out of a catnap until the Town Car coasted
to a stop outside her apartment building. Indulging in a yawn,
Simone thanked the driver, swung out, and strolled into her
building.

"A rooty-poot doorman don't mean shit to me. If you
want my black ass to leave, then you better call motherfucking S.W.A.T. Because I ain't leaving until that bitch drags her
scrawny little ass through that door."

Simone stood there in horror as Luscious Brown read the
riot act to Lewis, the normally bored but currently terrified
doorman.

Lewis glanced up with relief at the sight of Simone. "This
woman insisted on—"

Luscious stormed in Simone's direction. "Oh, this bitch
knows *exactly* what I insisted on."

Simone raised a halting hand. "This is *not* the projects.

This is a respectable apartment building with high community standards, and if you can't conduct yourself as something more than a common streetwalker, then I'll be forced to instruct my doorman to telephone the authorities."

"Well, bitch, I might be forced to put my foot up your bony ass!" Luscious shot back.

Simone stepped sideways to address Lewis.

Luscious moved right with her. "This ain't got nothing to do with him. This is between *us*. Now I'm tired of running you down to have the same conversation, okay? You are working my nerves, bitch."

Simone's mobile began to buzz. She glanced down to see that it was Kevon calling and picked up straightaway. "We have a situation here."

"I know, baby girl," Kevon answered thickly. "I'm about to roll up outside your building, so I hope it's a sexy situation."

"Don't tell me that's Kevon burning up your cell phone minutes!" Luscious screamed.

"You've got to be fucking with me," Kevon griped. "Is that Luscious Brown I hear talking shit in the background?"

Beyond disgusted, Simone slammed the phone shut and stomped outside onto the sidewalk.

Luscious followed in hot pursuit. "Bitch, don't walk away from me! I'm talking to you!"

Several car lengths away, Simone thought she could make out Kevon's Hummer limousine cruising toward the building. She narrowed her gaze to be sure.

Suddenly, Luscious was upon her again, this time pulling on Simone's arm and attempting to shove her down to the concrete. But her efforts were no match for Simone's Pilates-strong legs.

"Get your hands off me!" Simone cried.

Luscious continued to push, even as two fake nails popped from her fingers and clattered onto the sidewalk.

Passersby simply walked past the melee with little interest.

"Goddamn, Luscious! What the fuck are you doing?" Kevon shouted from his lowered limousine window.

Luscious stopped pushing Simone the moment Kevon's first syllable dropped and stalked toward the curb and the idle Hummer. "This ain't got nothing to do with you! This is between me and her!" She air-jabbed a finger in Simone's general direction.

"No, you got it all wrong," Kevon shot back. "What *I* got with her ain't got nothing to do with *you*. This woman's on TV. She ain't no girl from the block you can go running down. Damn! Now take your crazy ghetto ass back home and stop stirring up shit."

Luscious put hand to ample hip and poked out her lower lip. "If you want me home so bad, then give me a ride, hell."

"No, you need to sit your big ass on the bus and think about the stupid shit you did," Kevon snapped.

Simone watched the scene as if it were a bad movie, one that she would never even watch, much less play a role in.

As Luscious shuffled down the sidewalk muttering curses, Kevon leaned out of the window and tried to sweet talk her. "I'm sorry about that, baby girl. Come inside for a minute. Let me talk to you. I want to make sure my honey's all right."

Still dazed by the insane situation, Simone found herself sequestered inside Kevon's Hummer before she fully realized that she did *not* want to be there.

"Kevon, I don't know what we are doing or what we were doing, but I do know that it's over. Right here. Right now. I'm not putting up with any of this nonsense."

"It's all good, baby girl," Kevon said soothingly. "It's all good. I've handled things. Nothing like that will ever happen again."

"So you *do* know her," Simone accused. "She's not some crazy fan."

"Yeah, I know her . . . *and* she's a crazy fan." He laughed a little.

But Simone remained stone-faced. "Any man who wants to see Simone Williams, *only* sees Simone Williams."

"You're the only woman I'm seeing like that, baby girl," he assured her. "The Luscious Browns don't mean a thing." Kevon reached for an iced-down bottle of Cristal. "Now let's wet those sweet lips with some champagne."

Simone waved away the offer. "Now wait a minute. When I said, *only see Simone Williams*, that's precisely what I meant. There is no *like that* to seeing someone exclusively."

Kevon gave her a crazy look. "Do you plan on sucking my dick whenever I want a blow job?"

Simone lengthened her spine and stared back haughtily. "That's disgusting. I don't do that."

"Well, you sure are making a lot of demands for a woman who won't suck dick. Because I'm not giving that up. There are plenty of hos who'll do it just to say they did. But that's got nothing to do with you. Or us."

Simone had heard quite enough. "Correction—this has nothing to do with *me*. There is no *us*. At least not anymore." She moved fast to slip out of the limousine and onto the sidewalk.

What she saw first was the wheels of an SUV turning fast to jump the curb and career in her direction. What she saw last was Tommy Robb behind the wheel . . .

THE IT PARADE
BY JINX WIATT

Fill in the Blanks

Hell hath no fury . . . you know the rest, darlings. A certain mature morning chat show doyenne is working overtime to avoid the swinging ax. Rumors are rampant that number-crunching execs are adding up the viewer polls that reveal TV watchers would rather tune out than in whenever this half-century lady's on the screen. Ouch! How patient will the suits be? And how many lives does this snarling spinster cat have in the biz? Nine is the magic number. But some say she's already on number eleven.

25

Sutton

Sutton stared slack-jawed at the front page of the *New York Post*:

YANKEE ROBB KILLS BYSTANDER IN JEALOUS ROAD RAGE

New York Yankees superstar Tommy Robb has left the batter's cage for a jail cell after a jealousy-fueled road rage incident that left one pedestrian dead.

Witnesses say Robb was aiming for Simone Williams, a former actress/model and now a television talk show host on *The Beehive*, when his 2008 Cadillac Escalade struck Queens resident Luscious La Raison Verdeeka Brown on the sidewalk in front of the Upper East Side apartment building where Williams lives.

Robb and Williams were romantically linked before breaking up last New Year's Eve. Williams is now reportedly dating hip-hop mogul Kevon Edmonds, who led efforts on the scene to provide emergency assistance for the victim. Brown died hours later at Lenox Hill Hospital. The twenty-three-year-old is survived by one daughter, Princessia Purple Rain Shelton, and two sisters, Precious Quanticia Brown and Delicious Yvette Brown.

No official charges have been filed against Robb. At press time, the Yankee outfielder was awaiting arraignment. Blood alcohol level and drug test results are pending.

Sutton put down the newspaper and sipped slowly on her coffee as Joey and Olivia quietly did their hair and makeup work. She tapped a manicured nail on the ghastly headline. "Has anyone seen Simone this morning?"

Joey spoke up first. "She's still a little shaken up, but I think she'll be fine. Simone's a tough girl."

"A *lucky* girl, too," Olivia put in. "That could've just as easily been her in the hospital morgue."

Sutton cleared her throat. "Was Emma in makeup?"

Joey and Olivia traded meaningful glances.

"No, I haven't seen her," Joey said.

Sutton watched their reactions but said nothing. To say *The Beehive* set suffered from tension was the understatement of the year. Was Sutton on her way out? Had Emma quit for good? Who was being considered to fill the possible slots? The questions were piling up. But the answers were far less plentiful.

"Gorgeous suit," Joey remarked, carefully brushing a speck of lint from Sutton's Alpine white shoulder. "St. John?"

She nodded.

He caught her gaze through the mirror and smiled. "It becomes you. Very elegant."

"Maybe we should change my hair," Sutton suggested. "To better match the suit."

Joey played with some styles, entertaining the idea of putting it up, wearing it down, pulling it back. "I vote up," he said finally.

"Me, too," Olivia agreed. "You have such a pretty face and such gorgeous skin. You can pull it off. And believe me, not everyone can with the up-do." She laughed a little.

Sutton nodded her approval to Joey.

She was enjoying a whole new approach to life after contemplating a full bottle of Ambien. There had been the career Waterloo in Jay Lufkin's office. And shortly after that, the cruel reality of Scooter's true interest and the losing bet with his buddies that had predicated their first encounter. For a prolonged moment, the pills seemed like the least painful solution to her disappointments and humiliations.

But the shrewder aspect of Sutton's mind ultimately prevailed. She was not going to destroy herself over a loser like Scooter Betts. He was an uneducated barkeep with a metal bar pierced into his cock. Big fucking deal. So what if he made a fool of her? She caught on more quickly than he wanted her to, *and* she enjoyed some amazing orgasms courtesy of his impressive bedroom prowess. At the end of the day, she could hardly call it a total rip-off.

And she was not going to roll over and play dead on *The Beehive* for the White Glove executive pricks, either. Those poll-obsessed assholes had all the ingredients for a great show sitting in their laps, but they were too busy slaving over research data to realize it.

Had they even considered the overall concept for the show when they got a sudden hard-on for Paula Deen and bellied up an offer to her people? For starters, how would that woman's favorite macaroni and cheese recipe and cornpone family memories play against Finn's big city gay boy act and Simone's fashionista persona? Even the dumbest son of a bitch could predict certain disaster for that scenario.

And it was not until word leaked about Emma's decision to leave the show that Sutton allowed herself to realize the strengths the young journalist brought to the program. Her appeal to viewers could not be denied. The research was there to prove it. Sutton also had to admit that the girl's background was rock solid. She had the double college degree in broadcast journalism and political science, the fast ascent from local news field reporter to anchor.

The irony was not lost on Sutton. She had been consumed with irrational hatred for Emma, obsessed with the idea of forcing her out. But now she could see that *The Beehive* needed her. Emma Ronson was the star. Sutton could admit that now. And the show needed her presence, competence, and universal appeal. Without it, the whole enterprise could implode. For the sake of the bigger picture, Sutton could link arms with a fellow newswoman and get the job done. The situation could be worse . . . say, a reality bimbo of the Elisabeth Hasselbeck variety sitting beside her. Jesus Christ. *That* would be torture.

The days of Sutton blaming Emma for Garrison leaving her were over. In hindsight, her animosity had been such a spurned woman cliché. As a general rule, Sutton had such impatience for other women who hated the sluts their husbands and boyfriends slept with yet somehow found a way to forgive these cheating bastards. And she had succumbed to the same emotional weakness.

But that was the past. Sutton had clarity now. It had barely arrived in the nick of time. There was much work to be done and many fences to mend in order to set *The Beehive* on the proper course for continued success. And together, Sutton felt certain that she and Emma could unite into a reckoning force when it was time to do battle against Jay and the White Glove executives for the greater good of the show.

Enough with the goddamn research and ridiculous cater-
ing to the whims of viewers! They would never build the
perfect program that way. Television success was like lightning
in a bottle, nearly impossible to manufacture and replicate. There
was a reason why *Friends* soared to phenomenal heights while
every cloned sitcom about twentysomething singletons failed
fast.

Sutton had been knocking around the business for more
than twenty-five years. She had learned a thing or two during
that tenure. Now it was time for her to stop acting like a
horse cunt and teach these fuckers what she knew before
everything came crashing down around them.

As Joey and Olivia fluttered around her, Sutton continued
to observe their tense posturing and secret glances. She felt
certain that *something* was going on. And it had nothing to do
with the general state of unknown plaguing *The Beehive* set.

"What is it?" Sutton demanded.

Joey and Olivia traded wild-eyed looks.

"The two of you obviously have some piece of news that
you don't want to tell me but can't wait for me to find out."

Joey's gaze fell onto the *New York Post*.

Sutton snatched the tabloid and began whipping through
the pages on a mad search for whatever she had missed. And
suddenly there it was, with a photograph no less.

AGING PUBLISHING MAGNATE ECHOES HEFNER
IN STEAMY ROMP WITH JAPANESE STARLET
TWIN SISTERS

Self-proclaimed "magalog king" Garrison Friedberg, 64, could be a walking testimonial for the ED
drug industry. Sources claim he's scoring with not
one but two Japanese starlets. Last night the publisher cut a swath through Manhattan's trendy night-

club scene flanked by reality show phenoms Mio and Mako Kometani, twin sisters who have hit it big stateside with the Oxygen network reality show *Deep Inside M&M.*

"They were *all* over each other," a source told the *Post.* "Totally making out. It was disgusting. I couldn't tell if they needed to get a room or call an ambulance."

Friedberg's spokesperson dismissed the romance rumors, insisting that the publisher's interaction with the twins is exclusively related to a magalog launch called *M&M Forever,* which will pull double duty as a lifestyle magazine and catalog for Mio and Mako Kometani products.

Sutton stopped reading, plopped the tabloid back onto the counter . . . and started to laugh. It was real laughter from the gut. Once she started, she could not stop. Her stomach hurt. Her eyes watered. And the physical and emotional release felt fantastic. In fact, it was almost—but not quite—better than sex with Scooter.

Joey and Olivia seemed to be waiting for the other Jimmy Choo to drop, as if her laughing attack was due to give way to a crying jag any moment.

"You can relax," Sutton managed to say. "I'm not crazy. It's just so . . . *ridiculous.*"

"It really is," Olivia agreed.

Joey chuckled and shook his head. "What is it with straight guys and twins? I mean, it's kind of gross, you know?"

"I've known Garrison to do a lot of things," Sutton ventured quietly, as if sharing some essential bit of inside information.

Joey and Olivia listened in awe.

"But I've never known him to think with his dick when it comes to business. I think that's a sign the poor man is losing it. Those imbeciles are already forty-five seconds into their fourteenth minute."

Joey tilted his head. "I wonder if they make him listen to their CD. You know, like as foreplay or something."

Olivia giggled. "Well, if he can still perform after listening to *that*, then he's better than any man half his age."

Sutton smiled, quite satisfied with herself. Garrison was the laughingstock now. What a glorious turnaround. "Okay, kiddos. Finish me up. I need to have a heart-to-heart with Jay before the show."

Joey made some final adjustments to Sutton's upsweep as Olivia worked fast to touch up her eye makeup. "All done," they announced in perfect unison.

Sutton rose up from the chair, smoothed out the skirt of her St. John suit, and gave herself one final once-over. She looked sophisticated. She looked confident. And she looked *fifty*. But most of all, she looked fucking fabulous.

Jay was engrossed in a telephone conversation when she slipped inside his office. He nodded, raising a finger to indicate that he would only be a minute. "Thanks for the call. I'll pass the word upstairs . . . And to you as well." He replaced the receiver and gave Sutton a meaningful look. "That was the official decline from Paula Deen's camp."

Sutton betrayed no reaction, which was quite easy to do since she felt no sense of real relief. *The Beehive* was hers to mold, and nobody was going to step in and take her place. God would not allow it. This was her destiny.

"Welcome back," Jay said. "You look like a million dollars."

"Only a million?"

"Okay, one point five."

"Cheap bastard."

Jay smirked.

Sutton slid into the seat opposite his desk and crossed her legs. "What's happening with Emma?"

"You'll be pleased to know that she quit. It's not official yet. I'm still hoping that she'll reconsider." He splayed open his hands in a helpless gesture. "But she's not here today."

"Believe it or not, I'm not pleased at all."

Jay's brow shot up in surprise.

"What's her issue?" Sutton asked.

"*The Beehive* is too soft. Emma wants more substance."

"She's right."

"The research—"

"Fuck research," Sutton cut in. "It's based on attitudes that can change faster than you can act on the information. *Research* told ABC to put Regis in prime time four nights a week with that millionaire bullshit, and then the network was on life support until *Desperate Housewives* came along. The show *is* too soft. Those Kometani twits have served their purpose. Dump them. And I'm not saying this because they're fucking Garrison Friedberg. I'm saying this because by the time viewers get sick of them, it'll be too late. Use your instincts, Jay. You used to stage talk shows in your backyard as a kid. Stop using surveys, and start relying on those impulses. The public needs to be aware of *The Beehive* even if they're not watching it. That's real success. Look at *The View*. It's never been hotter. We'll never get there on the track we're on. Giving airtime to those Japanese whores giggling about who was supposed to clean up the dog's shit will never generate the kind of heat to make it to the next news cycle."

Jay gave her an impressed nod. "You're talking like a creative consultant."

"*Co*-creative consultant," Sutton shot back. "I'll share the responsibility with Emma. I want an extra carrot to offer when I convince her to come back."

"You're serious."

"I've been kicking around for almost three decades, Jay, and I've only made it to the middle. Never the top. But this is my chance to get there and prove all those motherfuckers wrong. I can't do it alone, though. I need Emma. She's the star. I'm fine with that. But I've got the experience of a veteran. And she needs that, too."

"Get her back," Jay said. "We'll do it your way."

Sutton challenged him with a steely gaze. "Do you mean that?"

"Absolutely."

"Then let's start today. Send Simone home. Her first day back after this horrifying incident should coincide with a big one-on-one interview. She hasn't really connected with viewers yet. That's a golden opportunity."

"Done." Jay grinned. "Want to know a secret?"

Sutton looked at him expectantly.

"I low-balled the Paula Deen offer."

She laughed a little. "You sneaky son of a bitch."

THE IT PARADE
BY JINX WIATT

Fill in the Blanks

Popular girls rule. Ask any high school cheerleader. She'll tell you that she runs the world. Daytime chat's newest blonde princess should give the same answer. All the beautiful cohost had to do was stomp her feet to get those silly Tokyo twins banned from her show. But it hasn't been quite so easy for her to get the man of her dreams. The newly unemployed prince left her to marry another. But now he's available again. Does this mean Missy High Q Rating has a real shot at fairytale romance?

26
Emma

"So what are you going to do?" Delilah asked. "I'd love to see you join the writing staff on *Laugh Track*. I mean, God knows the room could use another vagina." She put a comforting hand on Emma's knee. "But you're just not funny. Never have been."

Emma flicked her hand away good-naturedly. "I'm well aware of my shortcomings in the humor department."

Delilah laughed. "I still can't believe you quit. This was a huge career move, and you don't have anything else lined up. Can you afford to quit? What did your agent say? Hey, maybe you can get your old gig back at *Today in New York!*"

Emma shook her head. "They promoted Mandy Gabler."

Delilah made a face. "Her nostrils are too big. I bet they'd take you back in a heartbeat. Call them."

Emma sighed deeply, revealing more angst about her decision than relief. "I should probably just take some time. Maybe I could travel. I've always wanted to go to India."

"You're calmer than I'd ever be in this situation," Delilah said. Her voice rang with a quality equal parts praise and you-must-be-crazy. "I haven't been without a job since I was eleven. I went from babysitting to scooping ice cream to waitressing to more waitressing to still more waitressing until I got the nod from *Laugh Track*." She paused a beat. "God, I'm so under-qualified. I can't do anything but balance heavy trays of food and write fart jokes."

Emma laughed.

"It's true!" Delilah insisted.

Emma tripped off into a faraway place where the doubts began to mount. "Do you really think I was too impulsive?"

Delilah shrugged in answer. "Who am I to say, really? It was impulsive in that you hadn't planned on doing it. But it was also gutsy and highly principled."

"Thanks for saying that." Emma eased back against the sofa. Here she was, hibernating in her apartment in the middle of the afternoon, still in her silk pajamas and pink Uggs . . . and unemployed.

"But there is tape of you sitting down for an interview with the Kometani sisters," Delilah pointed out lightly. "So you'll never be Christiane Amanpour. You do realize that, right?"

Emma flipped her off. "Yes, bitch, I realize that. Anyway, that's not what I want. I don't mind the lighter segments. They can be fun. At the end of the day, though, I'm a serious girl. And I want to talk about serious issues." She let out a frustrated groan. "There's no reason why the show can't do both. But it seems to be heading in another direction."

"Yeah," Delilah snorted. "It's speeding straight into lobotomy central. The first ten minutes of *Regis and Kelly* can be more intellectually stimulating."

"Well, it's not my problem anymore," Emma said with a dismissive wave of her hand that belied the twisted feeling in the pit of her stomach.

The telephone jangled.

Emma glanced at the cordless, then back to Delilah. "Maybe CNN has heard the news." She picked up.

It was Gregory, the doorman, announcing a visitor.

"Who is it?" Emma asked.

"Sutton Lancaster."

Emma's heart lurched in her chest. She clutched her palm over the mouthpiece and hissed the latest development to Delilah.

"Ooh—can I stay and watch?" Delilah whispered. "God, I wish you had a lily pond. It would be so Alexis and Krystle from *Dynasty*."

Emma rolled her eyes. And then she cleared her throat. "Thanks, Gregory. Please send her up." She clicked off the phone and just sat there for a moment, nervous as hell. Finally, she turned back to Delilah. "Go hide in the bedroom and write a fart joke or something." Emma stood abruptly, wondering if she should change clothes. "I never expected this. What do you think she wants?"

"Maybe she wants the two of you to join forces and have Garrison Friedberg killed."

Emma's mind was racing. Maniacally, she glanced around the spotless apartment. There was nothing to straighten up. She had recently embarked upon a cleaning binge to pass the time. Even the baseboards had been scrubbed clean.

Suddenly, there was a dramatic knock on the door.

Emma motioned for Delilah to disappear into the bedroom.

"Watch out for her nails. I bet she's one of those women who scratches when she fights."

"Just go!" Emma half-whispered, half-shouted, now fully exasperated with her friend, as the anxiety over the imminent confrontation reached a near panic-inducing peak.

She walked over to the door. She took a deep breath. She opened it.

Sutton Lancaster stood primly on the other side, resplendent in her flawless St. John suit and Jimmy Choo heels. "Hello, Emma. I'm sorry for dropping by unannounced. Thank you for seeing me."

Emma gestured for her to come inside. "I wasn't expecting visitors." She waved a hand up and down her attire. "Clearly."

Sutton managed a polite grin. "I'm not very good at apologies, so I'll make this short. No matter, I certainly owe you one."

Emma could hardly believe the words that were being spoken.

"I've treated you terribly. I was unprofessional, petty, childish, and cruel. And I hope you can forgive me."

Emma merely stood in stunned silence.

Sutton's gaze turned expectant. "Well . . . *can* you?"

"Oh, yes, of course!" Emma finally erupted. "I'm sorry. Yes, apology accepted. It means so much that you came here to say this. Really, it does. I've always—"

"Be warned. If you say admired me since you were a little girl, then I'm going to push you out the window."

Emma smiled and stopped talking.

"We have similar concerns about *The Beehive*," Sutton went on. "So I'm asking you to come back . . . with the added title of co-creative consultant. We'll share the responsibility. I want you to work with me to make this show the kind of program we both know that it can and should be."

"You're serious," Emma murmured, still shocked by the seemingly impossible turn of events.

"Yes, I am," Sutton assured her. "If it's a topical issues segment that you want, then we'll add it. Maybe we can develop a point-counterpoint segment for the two us. You strike me as somewhat of a libertarian. I tend to be more conservative. Or we could take a generational approach. There are so many options. And we have the green light from Jay to experiment without interference. I know that we can make *The Beehive* something to be proud of, a show that's worthy of our credentials and journalistic experience."

"*Our?*" Emma repeated, her hand falling to her heart. She was beyond apoplectic.

Sutton's voice dropped an octave. "You have it all, Emma. You're so much more together than I was at your age. Frankly, I find it somewhat intimidating."

Emma laughed a little. "*You* find *me* intimidating."

"Not standing right here in those stained pajamas, no," Sutton said. "But in theory, yes. Sometimes I feel like a woman way past her prime when you're on the set."

Emma shook her head in disbelief. "But you've covered everything—Reagan's assassination attempt, wars, 9/11. I feel like a little girl playing dress-up next to you."

Sutton reached out and took both of Emma's hands in hers. "Enough of this shit. Are you coming back or not? And before you answer, know that those Japanese tramps will never darken the studio door again."

"Yes!" Emma squealed, practically jumping up and down. "I'll come back!"

Sutton smiled.

It was not a huge smile. But it was big enough to fill Emma's heart with pride. "Oh, God! Forgive my manners. Can I get you anything? Some coffee, perhaps?"

Before Sutton could answer, Emma's BlackBerry began to vibrate on the coffee table.

She started to ignore it for now, but a strange and certain instinct told her not to. "Excuse me—just for a moment." Emma dashed over to see DEAN PAUL CALLING on the screen.

She hesitated. Her stomach did a somersault. And finally, she picked up. "Hello?"

The first sound Emma heard was the blood-curdling wail of a baby . . . then came Dean Paul's distressed voice. "Emma, it's me. I'm with my daughter. Tilly's out of town. She won't stop crying. I think something's wrong. Do you know anything about babies?"

Emma was instantly taken aback. She had never heard Dean Paul sound so vulnerable. "Where are you?"

"At our . . . at Tilly's place in Tribeca. I don't know. I'm freaking out here."

"Okay, just stay calm. I'll be there as soon as I can."

"Thanks."

Emma disconnected the call and sucked in a deep breath.

"Is everything okay?" Sutton asked.

"I hope so," Emma murmured. "A new father alone with a baby for the first time. It's probably nothing serious."

Sutton displayed zero interest in the situation. It was clear that she did *not* do children. "I'll leave you to your crisis then." One beat. "And I'll see you on the set tomorrow."

"Definitely," Emma said. She waited for Sutton to leave, then dashed into her bedroom to get dressed, filling Delilah in on the latest developments as she threw on a pair of skinny Paige jeans and a distressed Juicy Couture hoodie, stepped back into her Uggs, dashed out the door, and raced downstairs to hail a cab, feeling every bit of the panic that she heard in Dean Paul's voice.

Emma called him back.

"Hey." One word. And yet his voice was still shaky. In the background, Cantaloupe continued to wail, only this time it sounded like a struggle.

"I'm on my way," Emma announced.

"I think she's getting worse," Dean Paul said.

Emma took great measures to keep her voice calm. "It sounds like Cantaloupe is having trouble breathing. You need to call an ambulance. It might not be necessary, but it's better to be extra-cautious. The nearest hospital is St. Vincent's. I'll meet you there. Don't panic. She's going to be fine. Now hang up and call."

"Okay."

Emma waited for the click. And then she exhaled deeply. "Forget the Tribeca address," she told the driver. "Take me to St. Vincent's Hospital on West Eleventh."

The ride there seemed interminable. Traffic was slow moving, but thankfully, it was early enough in the afternoon hour to bypass total gridlock.

Emma paid the fare, vaulted out of the taxi at the emergency entrance, and rushed the information desk, keeping her eyes on red alert for any sign of Dean Paul. "Has Dean Paul Lockhart checked in?"

The attendant did not share Emma's distress. She glanced up wearily. "They just went back. Are you the mother?"

Emma hesitated. Amazingly, saying no would not have bothered her. But she nodded yes to avoid any further delays.

"Follow him," the attendant said, pointing to a handsome young black man in blue scrubs halfway down the corridor.

Emma rushed to catch up and discovered Dean Paul in one of the private examining rooms, pacing nervously as a female doctor hovered above Cantaloupe.

The doctor looked up. "It's a bad case of strep. I've never seen a throat as red as this. She has some open sores that are making it hard for her to swallow. I'll prescribe a round of antibiotics and some Prednisone. She'll be just fine."

Dean Paul breathed a sigh of relief and reached out for

Cantaloupe's hand, which promptly gripped his index finger and held on for life. He smiled in a way that she had never seen before. It was pure love.

Emma was moved by this vision of him, so sweet, so perfect, so beautiful. But she was even more moved by her own reaction to it. The truth—she was happy for him.

And in that glorious moment, Emma Ronson opened up her heart, and she set Dean Paul Lockhart free.

THE IT PARADE
BY JINX WIATT

Fill in the Blanks

If there's one place rich and trendy New Yorkers adore, it's a hot and swanky club that keeps them *in* and the bridge-and-tunnel crowd *out*. Tongues are wagging about a new VVIP (that's not a typo, darlings; it's double the very) haunt that will have the imprimatur of America's newly single Prince and America's Best Gay Friend. Suspicious talk has swirled about these two being secret partners. Is the about-to-go-public business announcement a cover-up or a shame-on-you moment for dirty minds?

27
Finn

Dean Paul was naked, flat on his back, but barely visible through the steam. "I'm still crashing at your place, we work out almost every day, and now you're suggesting that we go into business together? People are going to talk." His voice boomed over the hissing jets.

Finn forced himself to look away. No good could come from staring too long. "People are going to talk about what?"

"About us."

"And what will they say?"

"That we're . . . you know . . . a couple. I don't care. But I just don't want you to hear that kind of gossip and possibly get your hopes up."

The jets halted as *hopes up* ricocheted in the Crunch steam room.

Finn hung his head low in the wet heat. "Sometimes I wonder."

"What's that?"

"Whether it's my hope or your latent fantasy."

Dean Paul's laugh was cocky. "Yeah, right. You wish."

"You bring it up all the time. Maybe it's your wish."

"They don't come off the hetero assembly line any straighter than me."

"The fact that you just said that might indicate otherwise."

There was a long stretch of silence.

"You guys think everyone is gay," Dean Paul said, finally. "Name a hot celebrity, and there's been a rumor floated that he's gay—Brad Pitt, Matthew McConaughey, Tom Brady, the list goes on. I'll say this much—you're an optimistic bunch."

"You're ridiculous," Finn said wearily.

"Am I?"

"*Yes.* And by the way, aren't you the one who keeps insisting that George Clooney is gay?"

"He's never been married," Dean Paul reasoned.

"Oh, well, there you have it, because every man who's married—or ever has been married—could never be gay. And by the way, dumbass, George Clooney *was* married once."

"Why so touchy?"

Finn lifted his head and tossed Dean Paul an annoyed look, so annoyed that he zeroed in on the man's eyes, never once feeling tempted to steal a glance south. It was a baby step toward mitigating the crush. "It's hard not to be touchy. You're such a frustrating son of a bitch."

Dean Paul stood up to hook his towel around his waist, maintaining eye contact, practically daring Finn to look.

Finn was resolute, staring eye to eye like a tractor beam.

Dean Paul stepped down to join him on the first row. "I just like fucking with you."

"It's a bit cruel."

Dean Paul looked over at him in complete surprise.

"It is."

"*Cruel?* That's a little dramatic, don't you think?" He paused a beat. "Well, now that Tilly's out of the picture, maybe I should look up some of the old buddies she made me ditch. I'm not going to trade one moody bitch for another."

Finn experienced a flash of anger. "God, you're such a prick!" He rose up and started for the door. His hand was on it when he halted and spun around. "Why do you play these fucking mind games with me? You know my feelings for you are complicated. You know that. I try to be a platonic guy friend. I try like hell. And the only time I don't succeed is when you taunt me with this bullshit. You dangle the idea of something more out there. You tease me by stripping down in this steam room when you could just as well keep your goddamn towel on. And then you threaten to take all your toys and go home. The other day you were moving to Miami. Now you're ditching me to go back to your straight friends. How can you call me a bitch? *You're* the bitch. Jesus Christ, you play more games than a woman!"

Dean Paul shook his head. "You're too high maintenance, man. I can't be emotionally responsible for you."

"Are you fucking kidding me?" Finn raged. "You couldn't be emotionally responsible for a rescue dog! It took Cantaloupe almost dying for you to realize that she was actually a child! If you're attracted to a woman, chances are you'll marry her! God! You put out this notion that I should be more laid back like one of your old dopey buddies, but you don't treat me like one of those guys. So what happens is I end up acting like your stupid boyfriend. And you benefit from that. I'm overly thoughtful. I wait around for your calls and texts. I drop everything when you say go. You *know* this. And you play into it just enough to keep me going because it's good for you. Well, you know what, asshole? It's not good for me anymore. I'm done."

The hiss of the steam jets started up again.

And then Finn walked out. He occupied himself in the city for several hours—browsing the bookstores, taking in a matinee, shopping in SoHo. When he got back to the apartment, it was eerily empty. Dean Paul had packed his things and left his key on top of the bar.

He was gone.

For the next few weeks, Finn channeled all the energy that had gone toward Dean Paul into his new venture—Sacred. His dream was to make it *the* VIP nightspot of the moment.

Amazingly, he found a perfect 2,000-square-foot space in Chelsea. A high-end custom denim boutique had gone out of business in the middle of a lease, and Finn managed to broker a good deal.

Finn fancied himself the next Amy Sacco, the high priestess of the Manhattan hot scene with exclusive velvet rope destinations like Lot 61 and Bungalow 8. But he envisioned Sacred taking exclusivity a radical step beyond.

People who passed through the doors would be paid members. And not just anyone could write a check. They would have to be invited. *Sorry, Benji.* He also imagined a Sacred membership Internet-based social network accessible by secret password only. My Space and Facebook were for the masses. Finn had secured the URL sacredonline.net for a privileged few. That way members could cyber chat about goings on at Sacred without undesirables horning in.

On the strength of Finn's kick-ass business plan—and his unexpected success on *The Beehive*, his parents agreed to loosen the reins on his trust fund, though only enough to front the initial capital in his dream venture. He would still need other investors.

Finn's notoriety got him meetings with several cash-rich

potential partners. But it did *not* close the deal. Most of them gave him lip service on the frightening mortality rate of nightclub ventures. "It's a high risk business with a short life-span," one lawyer told him. "You need more than a hip idea."

Deep down, Finn truly knew that he had more than that. Sacred would be a slam dunk. With a high membership fee, fifteen-dollar drinks, two-hundred-fifty-dollar bottle service, and regular patronage, investors could be paid regular distributions of both equity and debt service faster than Tara Reid could say, "Another round, please."

Unfortunately, few believers were out there. So many startup entrepreneurs had been burned on the sex appeal of co-owning a hot nightclub that ultimately went bust. After being told no again and again, Finn wondered if he would ever be able to make a go of it.

And then a courier knocked on the door to deliver an envelope. There was a check inside for the exact amount he needed to move forward. Attached to it was a note:

> *I want in. At last, you can finally call me your part-ner. Just kidding . . .*
>
> Dean Paul.

Finn smiled. There was just no getting rid of the adorable bastard. And he secretly didn't want to. He hoped the unrequited feelings would go away. But for right now, at least, it was what it was.

THE IT PARADE
BY *JINX WIATT*

Fill in the Blanks

Has talent gone the way of the cassette tape and VHS format? Can you even find it anymore where celebrity is concerned? For example, take our favorite Black American Princess, she of the dim-bulb talk show banter asides, not-quite-there modeling career, blink-and-you-miss-her stints as an actress, and bad choices in boyfriends. Now what's put her on the fame radar is almost getting run over and spending herself into debtor's prison. I give up, darlings!

28
Simone

"What went through your mind?" Emma asked gently.

"That I was going to die," Simone said. "Honestly, I thought it was over for me." Tears welled up.

Emma reached out for her hand and clasped tight in a gesture of support. "I can't imagine how frightening that must have been."

The studio audience was riveted.

"It's strange," Simone continued, regaining her composure. "It wasn't fear that I felt the most . . . it was regret. I thought about my father, who died when he was only forty-six. I thought about my mother, whom I haven't spoken to in years. I thought about the bad choices I made to get in—and even worse *stay* in—a relationship with this *person*." She paused. "You know, it's amazing how much can go through your mind in a matter of seconds."

"It sounds like this incident changed you," Emma ventured.

Simone considered the statement. "I think it did. Profoundly. I saw Tommy's car jump the curb, and it downloaded in that instant that my relationship with myself was so . . . *flawed*. I chose the wrong guys—or let them choose me. I didn't respect the role of money in my life. I didn't honor my relationship and responsibility to my family. I thought I was going to die, and I had this horrible sense that I'd gotten everything wrong." She looked out at the audience. "And let me say for the record that I realize how incredibly lucky I am. A woman died that day. And she left behind a little girl who will grow up without a mother. That's the biggest heartbreak."

"Did you ever have any suspicions or fears that Tommy Robb might react this way?" Emma asked.

Simone shook her head. "Maybe I should have. The warning signs were there from the very beginning. He was controlling and possessive and verbally abusive. When we broke up, I felt stalked to a degree, but I felt helpless. He could just autograph a baseball and get out of almost anything. And he always had a girl hanging on his arm, so people thought I was the crazy ex-girlfriend instead of the other way around. It was terrible. If I had to do it all over again—and this is my advice for all girls out there—forget athletes and date an accountant!"

The audience laughed and clapped their approval.

Emma smiled and took Simone's hand again in a show of sisterly solidarity. "We can't wait to have you back tomorrow in *The Beehive* where you belong. But so much has been written about this tragedy—"

"Most of it is completely bogus," Simone cut in.

"Exactly. And we wanted our viewers to get the truth straight from you."

Simone gave Emma a wry look. "There's a lot of truth about me heading their way this week."

Emma smiled. "That's right. Simone has courageously agreed to be the first subject of our new Debt Makeover series, which will put consumers in financial crisis under the hot lights of a lifestyle coach, credit expert, forensic accountant, and retirement planner. That's later this week. Stay with us. We're coming right back with new country and pop sensation Taylor Swift."

Simone breathed an extended sigh of relief.

"You were wonderful!" Emma gushed. "Brave and honest and so relatable. You should feel proud."

Simone beamed as Jay gave her two enthusiastic thumbs up. For the first time the show had debuted, she felt like she belonged, like she had carved out a place uniquely her own, just as Sutton, Emma, and Finn had. It was a glorious feeling of accomplishment, relevance, and a new way of being.

She made a beeline for her dressing room and walked in just as her cell phone started to ring. Rushing to retrieve it atop the cluttered vanity, Simone saw that it was Tilly, no doubt calling about the live interview that had just wrapped. She hesitated, wondering if she was in the mood, then reluctantly picked up.

"Michael is going positively *mad!*" Tilly exclaimed before Simone could even peep out a greeting.

"Who's Michael?"

"My agent!" Tilly roared. "I told you that I'd put in a word, and he's been waiting for this interview to air to assess you as a potential client. And, well, now he thinks *I'm* brilliant for suggesting you to him in the first place. But he thinks you have *loads* of potential. He wants to scoop you up right away and start taking you around to publishers."

Simone's stomach did a series of little flips. "Publishers? What for?"

"To get you a book deal! What else?"

"But I don't know how to write!" Simone exclaimed.

"Oh, please, you don't have to know how to do that.

They'll find you a ghost writer. Trust me. All you have to do is gab with them over coffee or something. They'll do the rest."

"Tilly, I—"

"Simone, Michael is waiting for your call. And let me put this in proper perspective for you. He doesn't wait on many calls. People wait for *his* calls. He's one of the best, and he can get you out of this financial mess you've gotten yourself in. You kicked Kevon Edmonds to the side, so it's all up to you now. Just say, 'Thank you, Tilly,' and take down this number. I have to run. Cantaloupe's wardrobe stylist is due here any minute, and we have to pick out a new ski suit."

"This is crazy," Simone murmured, experiencing a stirring sense of excitement as she jotted down the nine digits. Her life was about to change. She could feel it.

THE IT PARADE
BY JINX WIATT

Fill in the Blanks

It was boldface names galore at the splashy opening for the hot new nightspot Sacred on Chelsea's club row. Certain NY haunts have a tough door. That's a given. Long lines, unbreakable velvet ropes, immobile bouncers, you name it. But the door at Sacred is downright brutal. Ask anyone who put their ego on the line to brave entry. Those mirror-image Japanese sisters were all dressed up with no place to go. And they were even accessorized by a megabucks publisher! To add insult to injury, the latest *Laugh Track* skit on the dim-bulb twins became the number one requested video on YouTube within hours of its posting. The goof on the girls is so popular that there's already movie talk. Expect them to be skewered on the big screen soon. Any coincidence that the parody writer's BFF claims the Asian imports' billionaire boyfriend as an ex? You tell me, darlings. Sacred is oh-so-exclusive that you can't even buy your way in. The annual membership fee for the sanctified pass is $2500, and one is offered that by invitation only. After being refused the opportunity to join, that ubiquitous hip-hop mogul threatened to open his own rival club across the street. Could it be a battle of the bars? We'll see. One certified Sacred member who never made it to the opening was that heiress/cosmetics model/mommy to a juicy melon. The poor recent divorcée had to evacuate her Tribeca apartment when her unit became infested with bedbugs. Yuck! She's taken up residence in a plush suite at the Chambers Hotel and has hired a small squadron of power attorneys to sue every resident in her building, the developer, the contractor, her real estate agent, the City of New York, and anyone else she can think of. Of course, the real story isn't who wasn't there but who was. That fabulous foursome from TV's *buzziest* daytime chat show dripped honey like a quartet of queen bees. And why shouldn't they? Life is sweet, darlings. Everybody's favorite Black American Princess was toasting the completion of her first book, a memoir on her days as a teen model, struggling actress, and girlfriend to that psycho baseball star still awaiting trial for that deadly hit and run. Rumor has it the big-dollar advance (high sixes, I'm told) cured all of this beauty's money woes. Helping

her celebrate was her gorgeous
blonde cohost, looking downright
cozy with her new beau, that too
yummy for words British actor she
met on the show when he stopped by
to promote his latest film. What a
dating service! Proudly watching
over the whole affair was the veteran
newswoman of the group. She's fifty,
still going strong, and late-life super-
success has inspired her to meta-
morphose from hellcat to pussycat.
Don't believe it? The story is that
she took pity on her down-on-his-
luck former boy toy and put in a
word to get the unemployed bartender a job serving Sacred drinks.
Too bad the creep got fired early
into the night for showing off his
tallywacker jewelry. The real kudos
of the evening went to morning television's funniest gay sidekick. The
Sacred concept was his brainchild
and bankrolled by a trust fund raid
and a business partnership with
America's prince. These buddies (not
the *Brokeback Mountain* kind, says
a source who *knows*) are on a roll
and planning a Sacred Miami, Sacred
Los Angeles, and Sacred Cabo. Hopefully, the ambitious plans won't be
derailed by the lawsuit just filed by
the witty TV boy's former boyfriend,
a con artist recently jailed for credit
card fraud who claims the entire
Sacred venture was his idea. Exes!
Like cockroaches and Cher, they

never seem to go away. Of course, the real tragedy is that television's most *buzz*-worthy jabber-jaw hour has gone from bitch-fest to love-fest. No catfights, no frigid silences in the makeup room, no complaints to the higher-ups about this one or that one. Just respect, friendship, and mutual admiration for all involved. Have you ever heard more depressing news? I give this show one more year, darlings. It has no hope of staying on the air with this kind of appallingly polite behavior.

29
Sutton

Once again, the German techno-inspired theme music commenced, followed by the announcer's booming voice.

"Ladies and gentlemen, you have officially entered *The Beehive*! Please welcome your hosts and winners of the 2008 Daytime Emmy Award for Best Talk Show Hosts . . . Sutton Lancaster . . . Emma Ronson . . . Simone Williams . . . and Finn Robards!"

Explosive applause and uproarious cheers greeted Sutton Lancaster as she emerged first from backstage, followed by Emma, Finn, and Simone.

She walked with pride, triumph, and renewed purpose. All those years of bottom-feeding at the local affiliates, of languishing in the middle ranks of network news. It was all worth it. For this.

Sutton assumed her perch at the center of the black Bee-Board table as her cohosts settled in around her. "*Daytime Emmy Award winner,*" she intoned sweetly. "You know, I still like the sound of that."

The crowd erupted with another thunderous ovation.

"Me, too," Finn enthused. "Announcer, please say it one more time."

The booming voice did the honors again.

"I should just have him record that and put it on my iPod," Finn remarked.

"We can't live on past glories, guys," Emma said easily. "Remember—we're only as good as our next show."

"But even if that one sucks, we're still Daytime Emmy Award winners," Simone put in. She raised a hand, unleashed a street-worthy, "Holla!" and accepted the high-fives of all of her laughter-collapsing cohosts.

"It's Monday," Sutton announced. "We just got the award Friday night, so we might be gloating a tiny bit."

"No, we're just being informative," Finn said. "Gloating is having this same conversation six weeks from now, which I'm sure that we will be."

"Now I have to say this," Sutton continued. "I'm sort of the den mother here. I'm a woman of a certain age."

"Fifty is the new forty!" Finn blurted.

"Thank you, dear," Sutton murmured. "But I've been knocking around this business for three decades. I've lived in countless cities, worked for dozens of affiliates, done a tour of duty on every network and cable news channel. I've seen talent and colleagues come, go, rise, and fall." Her eyes misted with tears. "But I've never had any better experience than what I've enjoyed on *The Beehive* here with all of you. I mean that from the bottom of my ratings-focused heart."

"The bitch is back," Finn sang.

There was an extended group hug. And then the show went on . . .

ABOUT THE AUTHOR

Kylie Adams is the author of ten previous novels, *Fly Me to the Moon, Baby, Baby, Ex-Girlfriends, First Kiss: The Bridesmaid Chronicles, Cruel Summer: Fast Girls, Hot Boys Book One, Bling Addiction: Fast Girls, Hot Boys Book Two, Beautiful Disaster: Fast Girls, Hot Boys Book Three*, and the *USA Today* bestsellers *The Only Thing Better Than Chocolate* (with Janet Dailey and Sandra Steffen), *Santa Baby* (with Lisa Jackson, Elaine Coffman, and Lisa Plumley), and *The Night Before Christmas* (with Lori Foster, Erin McCarthy, Jill Shalvis, Kathy Love, and Katherine Garbera).

Visit Kylie online at www.readkylie.com.